Under the Shadow's Eye

Dreamweaver Diaries
BOOK ONE

Eric Johnson

Broken Press
Table

To Laureena and Alec,

my inspiration and my future.

ACKNOWLEDGMENTS

This book would not have been possible without all the help and support I received from my family and friends throughout the years. My wife, who put up with my long hours of disappearing into the words that I create and who patiently listens to my excited non-sequiturs about characters and events she'd never heard of. My children, equally patient with my writing hours, inspire me to be the best that I possibly can. Bob and Lee, my folks, have supported my passion for writing for as long as I can remember and are probably my biggest fans. I love you all.

I want to give my sister and niece a special thanks for their commentary and critiques that allowed Isabella, the main character, to mature appropriately. Without them, this wouldn't have read as a young adult book. Jamison, my alpha reader, whose eyes were the first to land on my words and whose encouragement and critical eye helped me see my vision to the end.

UNDER THE SHADOW'S EYE

 PROLOGUE

The man stood at the edge of the forest and watched the child play. She didn't know he was there; she didn't even know she was there because it's hard to know where you are when you're dreaming. The man knew. He was here because of her— her and the other dreamers.

"I believe she is safe for now," the wolf said, standing next to him, his voice the tenor of the sound a heavy bag makes when dragged across a gravel road. "We need to go if you are going to see the council about this."

"I know Vígolfr," the man said, patting the wolf absently on the head. The two had been together for almost two decades, weaver and companion. Together they were powerful, efficient, and, when needed, brutal. He would go to great lengths to protect the girl and the thousands like her who traverse the bounds of the waking world and find their way to the dream world, but she was not like the others. She was his daughter, and when she was old enough, she would become like him. She was already showing the signs. The council, weavers who had given up their waking life to help maintain the dream world, didn't understand his connection to the waking world, his reasons for not giving it up when they offered him a spot. He hoped they would concede his current request, but his gut told him they wouldn't. There were rules.

"She will be safe," the wolf leaned against the man's leg. He knew how his weaver felt. He had made a promise, and a promise wasn't something he was willing to break, especially under these circumstances. He turned his face up to the man, the dark nose standing out against the bright white fur. "They wait on you."

With one final look at the girl as she got up and talked to the air, he wondered what she saw in her dream that he couldn't see but fought the urge to find out like he did when she was younger. This new independence was hard for him, but she was growing up, and nothing could stop that. Instead, he gave Vígolfr a decisive pat on the head and turned to disappear into the forest. They were traveling fast over land; his weapon of choice, a large sword, didn't slow him down in the dream world, though it would have gotten some strange looks in the waking world. He'd thought it odd at first, given the technology available to him in the waking world, to use such an archaic weapon, but when fighting the shadows, or his specialty the nightmares, what would be considered old-fashioned in the waking world just worked better. Most weavers and most hunters, the permanent residents of the dream world who help fight the shadows, use the simpler weapons.

Today, he didn't need to be particularly fast. He was close to his cabin, a bit of contraband grandfathered to his family because it predated the council and their shortsighted rules. In that cabin was a door that would lead him into the council's hall. That was the cost of keeping their family home in the dream world; they must be willing to do the council's bidding.

When he was eighteen and getting used to the idea of becoming a Dreamweaver, he bristled at the thought of being a slave to the council. He was just discovering what he could do and the intricacies of this world, but his grandfather was a serious man and didn't take his commitments lightly. It made sense that his companion was a magnificent stag that still stood proudly grazing with a group of local deer.

As he and Vígolfr ran the well-worn, familiar paths, the man marveled, as he did so often, at the similarities between the dream world and the waking world. It worked when you thought about it; the dream world was technically a manifestation of the collective dreams from generations of people. Still, there were rules here too, rules as immutable as gravity, rules that even the council, as much as they may not want to admit it, can't change.

The cabin, a place he'd known for the better part of two decades, left to him by his grandfather, was his home in the dream world. It should have been his father's, but something happened, and his father didn't come home one day. His grandfather visited the cabin that day and talked about sacrifice. The man had his own baby by then, and when his grandfather left, the man had cried. It was just as hard when the same had happened to his grandfather many years later, only that time it was one of the council who came to inform him, and that time he hadn't cried until the councilor left.

The door leading to the council's chambers was hidden in the bookcase because his grandfather enjoyed the whole situation's clandestine nature for all his dower appearance. On the days that the man caught his grandfather in a good mood with one of his complaints about being a slave to the council, the old man would say they were more like private detectives than slaves, and the secret door, kept secret even from the man until he was well into his twenties, was their office.

He understood now what his grandfather had been talking about. That was why he didn't jump when the council called, but he didn't ignore them either. He knew better. Often, they had information he needed to protect the helpless dreamers from the shadows and nightmares. A task that he was good at and enjoyed.

The council chambers were opulent with filigreed gold columns and held a large table made from an acacia tree found only deep in the southern deserts. Twelve dreamweavers sat on the council at any given time, and they were unquestioned. They ruled the dream world to a balanced peace.

"You took you time getting here," the council member sitting on the farthest left end of the table stood up and greeted the man. He towered over the man, broad-shouldered with arms as wide as a man's thigh. Close-cropped brown hair covered his head and flowed into an equally close-cropped beard. His face looked like it could be friendly if he smiled, but the man had never seen him smile once. "Come to my office. I have something to discuss with you."

"Councilor Harris—" the man said, exchanging a look with Vígolfr. He could tell the wolf was equally troubled because the council did its business in the open. They had always been transparent.

"Don't worry," an older woman from the fifth seat stood, her graying hair pulled up in a severe bun, contrasting sharply with her mocha-colored skin. Resting her hand on the back of her chair, she looked every bit the warrior the man had heard people talk about. The careless way she looked around the room before walking behind the other councilors who seemed contented to remain mute in whatever this was. She moved like water, flowing gracefully across the diadem where the council sat. As she moved to the door, her smile was a welcome change from the severity of Councilor Harris. She ushered the man and Vígolfr into the room and, following them in, shut the door behind the man, his shoulders tensed as they did when threatened. Feeling his unease, Vígolfr also moved with more sinewed grace, his muscles reading for a fight. Both knew the battle would not be here. You didn't fight with the council because they were the authority, and with authority, or because of it, came power, both perceived and real.

The councilwoman's companion, a ferret or a mink, the man never really could tell the difference, seemed the sense the change in their demeanor and crawled up onto the councilwoman's neck. Councilor Harris's companion, a brown bear, kept sleeping in the corner, not seeming to care about the others in the room. Secure in the intent of the meeting or in his strength to overcome whatever was in his way, the man wasn't sure which but knew that he didn't want to find out either.

"Oh, relax you two," she laughed lightly and made a shooing gesture at them with one hand, "My word Harris, those two are entirely so high strung lately."

Leaned against the wall, arms crossed in front of himself, Harris looked down at the man disapprovingly and grunted. That didn't help the tension any, so she continued as if they had, or perhaps she was so used to people listening that she didn't bother to notice.

"I swear, the two of you need to get over this," she absently waved her arm at the man and Harris, "this whatever it is before I get annoyed and do something about it myself." She pointed to a section on the map, far to the east. "I've heard some rumors lately that there is a shadow congress forming in this area."

"Shadow congress," the man ruminated for a moment, "I'm sorry, Councilor Merin, I don't think I've heard of that before."

"They are rare," she admitted, "the last one was just before the great purge, and some are talking about this new congress being a sign of things to come."

"The council believes in omens?" Vígolfr's gravely voice sounded even harsher when laughing.

"No," she shifted her sharp green eyes to the wolf who reflexively looked away, "but they do see a shift coming. We aren't the council of dreamers because we lack vision. There are shifting allegiances and rumors of some dark machinations. We've even begun enlisting the aid of some hunter clans through the region, the champion's group in particular. Personally, between us, I think some of the council are nervous."

"Paloma," Harris pushed himself from the wall, "do you think we should tell *him* that."

Shifting her gaze to Harris, who visibly deflated beneath it, she scoffed, "Councilor Harris is among the nervous ones to be quite frank."

"We shouldn't show the weavers dissection in our ranks," he grumbled, leaning back against the wall.

"I entirely agree, Oliver," she put an uncomfortable emphasis on his name, causing him to shift position, a reaction that seemed to satisfy her because she nodded and returned her attention to the man.

The man nodded, his shoulders relaxing, this was the reason for the closed door, the council was scared.

"Your family has been one of our staunchest supporters through the many changes in this world, and you are one of our top weavers. Your particular skill-set will be needed. I've already dispatched your old apprentice, Wren, to do the legwork. You and Vígolfr will do what you do best, cleanup."

"I prefer to think of it as protecting the dreamers," the man did not like being thought of as the cleanup crew. "That is what we are supposed to do, right?" The question was not one that needed an answer; it was more of a reminder. The man often found he needed to remind the council what mattered from time to time.

"And the dreamers won't be safe unless you help break up this shadow congress," she retorted.

"That's a long distance," the man traced his finger from the capitol to the spot the councilwoman had indicated, "I'll have to let my family know I'll be away for a while."

"Of course," she smiled what the man assumed was supposed to be a warm smile, but it looked more like she had just been forced to drink vinegar, "we understand." She looked at the map and then back at a note written on a piece of paper under that map. "Wren will be ready for you in a couple of days, so when you *do* come back, travel quickly."

The man left the council chambers, took the door back to the cabin, and went to check on the girl. When he got to the edge of the forest, he could see the coming dusk. With the darkness came the shadows, and with the shadows, danger. He wanted to wait for the girl to wake up before leaving the dream world, but he knew he couldn't. Time was short, and he still needed to break the news to his family.

 ONE

Isabella was in the darkness again. Surrounded by the plush hold of a soundless night, her pulse quickened. Something was wrong. She knew it was wrong. Moving her arms out on both sides. The darkness was pushing in on her again, and she tried to push it back, kicking with her legs and pushing at the suffocating darkness, trying to make room around her face so she could breathe. She tried to scream, but no sound would come out of her mouth. Her eyes darted around the folds of darkness surrounding her, pushing the air from her lungs by the increasing pressure. Frantically Isabella tried to grab anything she could get hold of. Although she could feel the darkness pushing in on her, her arms met with no resistance when they swung out. Her heartbeat surged in her ears, breaths coming short and shallow.

Panic rose from the pit of her stomach as she tried desperately to remember where she was and how she'd gotten there.

Without warning, her legs broke free of the suffocating darkness, and she kicked her bare feet in the cold night air. With the hope of escaping the crushing darkness now beginning to bloom, Isabella squirmed her body, trying to snake her way out of the hold she was in. Her knees were the next to emerge, cold despite the summer night. Sweat started beading on her forehead. She wasn't sure what was beneath her, but she hoped it was better than the crushing nothing she was in. By the time her waist broke free, the fact that her feet still hadn't found solid ground was starting to worry her, but anything was better than being suffocated, so she continued to wiggle her way free.

Once she could get her shoulder's out, she felt a rush of air as she dropped onto the hard-packed floor of a forest. Isabella looked up at a black pulsing mass puckered in the middle and slowly descending to the ground where she fell. The wind whipped up and, vacuum-like, began pulling the leaves and twigs off the floor around her in a whirlpool toward the darkness she'd just escaped. Each pulse of the darkness caused a storm of lighter objects in the air around her. Her long blond hair flew in her face, and she wiped it way, trying to hold it back with one hand as she frantically looked for an escape.

All around her, the ground sloped down into a dark forest. She felt the pull of the darkness on her nightgown, and sharp sticks dug into her as she knelt at the top of a now bare hill, the darkness only a few feet above her head. She stood up and hunching over against the pulling wind, her hair standing straight on end, pulled toward the sky. She picked a random downward direction and ran as quickly as she could. The slope beneath her seemed to grow steeper as she descended into the forest until she had no choice except running at full force or tumbling uncontrolled down the hill, and Isabella didn't like not being in control. No matter how fast she went, the darkness staying several feet behind and above her, sucking in the trees as it went.

Isabella was sure that she wasn't going to make it. Pangs of terror washed over her as each tree ripped from its roots, throwing dirt and sticks in her path. With each step, the ground grew steeper. At this point, she was almost falling down the slope. She looked over her shoulder, her breath coming in ragged gasps, sweat dampening her thin pajamas, and saw the darkness drawing nearer, pulsing and pulling her back. Then the ground fell out from underneath her, and the wind tore at her nightgown and her hair. Arms flailing, she screamed out for help as she fell through the void toward a river coursing through jagged rocks. She watched the rocks fly up toward her and screamed again before a different type of darkness surrounded her.

She lay in the darkness, her nightgown soaked in sweat, breath coming in quick gasps. The silence around her was absolute for a second before a second scream shattered her confusion. She rolled her eyes, sighed angrily, and put the pillow over her head. The same dream every night for almost a month now, basically the same, she reminded herself. Each time it was harder to escape. That wasn't even the worst part, now her baby brother had to share a room with her, and she kept waking him up. Waking him up meant—

"Izzy," a calm voice spoke to her doorway. "Sweetheart, are you alright?"

She pulled her covered over her head and tried to pretend she was asleep, but that was hard with her head under her pillow, and it wouldn't stop her father from coming in anyway. She'd already woken her brother up again. Isabella folded the covered down to her shoulders and extricated her head from under her pillow. She put her head down heavily, turned toward the wall, and grumbled, "Tucker's awake."

"Sweetie," the calm voice said again, "did you have a nightmare?"

"Daddy," a small groggy voice spoke from across the room. "Daddy, sister sad?"

"Just a nightmare, buddy, go back to sleep," the exhaustion evident in her father's voice even to Isabella as she worked through her frustration with everything. It was bad enough that she kept having this nightmare, but now she had to deal with sharing her room with a baby.

"Daddy," the little voice asked again, "your bed, Mommy bed!"

"No, buddy," her father sighed, "go back to sleep."

"Okay," he whimpered.

"Baby girl, are you okay?" He sat on the edge of her bed and gently rubbed her back like he'd done when she was little. "Bad this time, eh?"

"I'm fine, dad," she said, but she didn't shrug his hand away, "go back to bed."

"Oh, sweetie, you're shaking," he patted her back reassuringly. "Do you wanna take a deep breath with me—"

"Dad," she shrugged his hand away this time and rolled over to face him in the darkness. "I'm not a little kid anymore. It was just a nightmare. I'm fine."

She saw him sigh in the darkness and knew the look he'd have on his face. He still saw her as a little kid, but she wasn't. The whole breathing thing had worked when she was little, it had helped calm her every time, but she didn't need that anymore.

"Daddy?" The little voice from across the room with tears clear in the halting word.

"If you're sure, Cricket," he patted her shoulder and stood up. "I just gotta get Tucker back down, okay."

She heard him get up and shuffle across the room to her brother's crib. She hated sharing her room with a baby, but her parents had insisted. A tree branch had broken through his window in the last storm, and it was taking so long to get it fixed, but she missed having her room all to herself. Tucker was a fun kid, as little bothers went. He was usually good to have around because she liked to blame things on him, but because he was learning how to talk a bit better, accusing him was getting more difficult. She still got away with it from time to time. But sharing her room was different. He had a crib, he wore a diaper, which meant a changing table, a smelly diaper trash pale thing, and his crying at bedtime. It also meant that when she had a nightmare, which was increasingly frequent lately, he would wake up and cry, then her father would have to come in and calm him down. She did not like that at all.

"Okay, buddy," her dad said as he finally got Tucker back down and covered up, "here's Leo. Now I'll just be across the hall while you go back to sleep. I love you, buddy. Night night."

He walked back over to Isabella's bed and sat on the edge. When he spoke again, his voice was quiet in hopes of not disturbing her brother. "They're getting worse, aren't they?"

Isabella turned toward the wall. His hand patted her back and rubbed soft circles around her spine. She dropped her shoulders and rolled back over onto her back to look up at him from her pillow.

"When is he going back to his room?"

"Not this again," her father sighed, "I told you, Izzy, we need to get it cleaned up first. The window we need is on backorder, and we're not going to have your brother sleeping in a construction site. I'll get the window replaced once it comes in, then you'll get your room back."

Isabella rolled her eyes in the darkness but didn't say anything.

"Dreams are getting worse, aren't they, Izzy?"

"This one was," she shuddered, remembering the black pulsing mass chasing her, "this was one of the worst."

"What was it about?"

"I don't want to talk about it."

"You sure," he asked, leaning down to kiss her forehead, "you know that helps sometimes."

"I'm fine, Dad."

"Okay, sweetie," he said, brushing the hair from her forehead. "You gonna be good going back to sleep?"

"Come on, dad," she rolled her eyes at the darkness, "it was just a dream, and I'm not Tucker." Her father was right though, the dreams had been getting worse and more often, but she hated to admit it. "Unless you're gonna let me go downstairs and watch tv?"

"No," he laughed, "it's two-thirty in the morning, goofball. You're going to go back to sleep."

"Want me to weave you a dream like I did when you were a little kid?"

"Seriously?"

"Hey, it worked back then," he chuckled warmly in the darkness.

"Back then, I believed in Santa Claus too."

"Hey now," his voice took a mock scolding tone, "don't you dare knock the man in red or no presents come Christmas, and won't you be sorry then."

Isabella rolled her eyes and smiled. Some people never seem to grow up, and her dad was one of them.

"Alright, Izzy," he lowered his voice as if he didn't want anyone else to hear him, "can you keep a secret?"

"What?"

"A secret," he repeated, "can you keep a secret, just between the two of us?"

"About what?" Her curiosity was piqued. Isabella loved secrets. She and her friends at school had tons of them. Boys they thought were cute, things that happened in class that they didn't tell their teachers, but a secret from her dad, especially a secret he wanted to share with her, seemed strange. She shifted her weight onto her elbow and leaned up so she could hear his quiet voice better. "What's the secret?"

"You can't tell anyone about this," his voice took on that tone he had when telling her to clean her room or eat her dinner. This was serious.

"Not even Tucker?"

"Not even Mom," he said. Now she knew this was serious, her father never kept secrets from her mom, and he had told her that keeping secrets from either of her parents was never right. "Pinky swear." He held his hand out, pinky extended.

"How old are you?" she laughed but played along and pinky swore.

He looked over his shoulder at Tucker, now sleeping in his crib, and turned back to Isabella, "I can make sure that you don't have another nightmare tonight," he began. "I can weave you any dream you want and put it right into your head, then when you go back to sleep, that is the dream you'll have. What do you think?"

"Okay, Dad," she rolled over to face the wall again.

"I used to do it all the time for you," he said, his voice both smiling and serious. "What do you want your dream to be?"

"Go back to bed," she said as she closed her eyes. "You must still be dreaming yourself."

"Doesn't really matter if you don't believe me. Humor me, okay? It'll help me sleep better."

"Fine," she rolled over onto her back and looked up at her father in the darkness, "but I'm not going to describe a dream to you."

"Okay," he said, "I'll try to make it something you might like." He moved his hands through the darkness mumbling something under his breath, and the dark room seemed to lighten a little.

"Alright, sweetie," he said when he was done, his hands still weaving through the darkness, "now close your eyes and turn your head to the left."

Isabella turned her head on her pillow, a smile plastered across her face, and her father moved his hands over her temple. With a quick breath, her father blew on her temple and spread his hands over her head. She felt a light pressure on her for a second, then nothing.

"Okay, now I'm going to take that nightmare out," he said, leaning back, "turn the other way." Humoring him, she turned her head, and he put his hands next to her head the sucked air through them. "Done."

"That's it?"

"Yup," he said, putting his fingers to his mouth as if he was taking something out and putting it in his pocket. "I'll get rid of this in the morning. Now, you go back to sleep and have that wonderful dream I just put together for you."

"Okay," Isabella could already feel the pull of sleep on her. "You're insane, you know that, right?"

"Goodnight, Busy Izzy," he said, standing up to leave the room. "I love you, Cricket."

"Love you too."

"I can't wait to hear all about that dream of yours in the morning."

"Okay," Isabella couldn't help but smile. She didn't buy any of this, but she did like it when her typically serious father was a bit goofy from time to time.

"And remember," he said as he stood in her doorway, "our secret."

"Our secret. Night Dad," Isabella shut her eyes and, after a little bit, drifted back off to sleep.

TWO

Izabella's father was sitting at the kitchen table, an ignored beer bottle in front of him sweating onto the table. "I know it's not ideal, hun, but it's business. Not like I have a choice in the matter,"

Her mother stood at the kitchen sink washing the dinner dishes, her back to him as she continued the conversation, "But Izzy's nightmares are still getting worse, you're in there every night for at least an hour trying to get Tucker back down when she wakes him up." She turned around and leaned against the sink, looking at her husband, "You know I don't do well with that little sleep."

"Izzy's fourteen; she's a big girl," he leaned back in his chair and looked toward the stairs, "she'll be okay while I'm gone, right Busy Izzy?" he called the last part out to Isabella, who had thought she was hiding just out of sight. "You might as well come in here. You've already heard what we're talking about."

Isabella walked into the kitchen, looking down at her feet. She didn't know how he always caught her when she was listening in on them, but it never failed; no matter how quiet she was, her dad always knew.

"Exactly how long have you been listening, Izzy?" her mother asked, annoyance clear in her voice.

"Not long," she said, shuffling her feet, "only a minute or two. I couldn't sleep." She knew that it was late and that her mother was already annoyed about her dad going away for business. Things had been tense all day, and after the past month of bad dreams, Isabella was on edge too, but at least now she knew why her mother seemed stressed out all day. "Tucker was snoring, and I couldn't get to sleep."

"Hun," her father said, "you know you need to be sleeping. Tucker doesn't snore that loudly."

"You're not in the same room as him."

"When is that window coming in anyway?" her mother asked. Isabella was glad to have the attention off of her for the moment, but she knew it was only temporary.

"Izzy, come here," her father patted a chair next to him. Happy that he was finally treating her like an adult, Izzy squinted as she came into the brightly lit kitchen and sat next to her father. "I think they said it would be here next week. You know, I could fix it." He got up and walked over to get a glass of water.

"If that were true, you would have trimmed the branch like I asked you to after the last storm," Isabella's mother snapped the towel at her father and smiled before going back to the dishes.

Shrugging, Izzy's father gave a conspiratorial grin before giving her a glass of water and picking back up his beer. "So, I'm guessing you heard?"

Izzy nodded, "You have to go away again."

"I know it's not great timing," her father put his hand on her shoulder and squeezed a little, "but I have to go for work."

"Why," she wined, "I thought you normally worked from home while we're in school? Can't you just work from home this week too?" He was already shaking his head before she finished speaking, but she forged on anyway, "I'll keep Tucker away from you while you work."

"I'm sorry, sweetie," he said, smiling sadly at her, "it's not that easy." He softened his voice a little as he spoke, "I know it sucks, and I don't want to be away from the three of you either, but there are some times, not often, but some times that I need to go away for my work. I don't get to pick them," he sighed at looked up at the back of her mother, "this is, unfortunately, one of those times."

"Fine," she leaned back in her chair and took a drink of water. She didn't want to care that her father was going away, but as much as she didn't want to admit it, her nightmares had always gotten worse when he was gone.

"Your mom will still be here. You can always call her when Tucker starts crying." He looked over at her mother as she turned off the water and came to the table.

"I'll come and get him back to sleep," she said, taking the seat on the other side of Isabella. "I just move a little slower than Dad when I'm asleep."

"But Dad," she said, "I need *your* help—" Isabella hadn't meant to say that, and her father raised his eyebrow. Feeling her cheeks warm, she plowed through, "with Tucker, I mean."

"Izzy," her mother said, "that's not fair to your father or me."

Isabella ignored her mother's plea; she was scared about the nightmares that had been growing in strength ever since she turned twelve. She had just been on the edge of one tonight when she woke up, Tucker breathing peacefully in his crib on the other side of the room. Sure, the comment about his snoring was a lie, but she didn't like to talk about the nightmares, especially to her mother. She didn't want to break her promise to keep her father's secret, not that she believed him anyway, but he had seemed pretty serious, and she was convinced that talking about her nightmares with her mother would lead to that. "You promised, Dad."

"Promised you what, Izzy?"

"That you'd keep the nightmares away," she couldn't believe she was saying it, but they were better when he was home. Isabella knew she was on dangerous ground, close to spilling his silly secret, but it was late, and she wanted to convince him to stay.

"Izzy, sweetheart," her mother said, resting a hand warmly on her back, "your dad would stay around if he could, you know that. Besides, aren't you a little too old to need your dad to fix your nightmares?"

"Besides, Izzy, you told me last night that you didn't need my help," her father was looking at her questioningly.

"You don't understand," Izzy huffed. She could feel the pressure building behind her eyes. "You can't keep them away like Dad does."

"Robert, what is she talking about?" She turned back to Isabella, "Sweetie, it's late. Why don't you head back to bed."

"You don't get it," Izzy was getting frustrated. All week she had avoided talking about her nightmares with her mother because she knew this would happen. "Just—never mind."

"Hunny?" her mom implored, the musical lilt in her voice pitched as she would do when her feelings were hurt.

"Because," Isabella closed her eyes and leaned her head back against the chair. She was getting tired and embarrassed and wanted this conversation to be over.

"Because why, honey?"

"Because Dad can weave dreams, and you can't," she blurted out. The moment the words left her mouth, Isabella felt like a fool. Her dad used to weave her dreams as a little kid, but he hadn't done it for years until last night. She was too old for that silliness anyway, but something about last night's dream and the one she knew she was about to have before she woke up tonight had gotten under her skin.

"Izzy," her mother said, raising her left eyebrow and smiling, "don't be silly. What do you mean your father can weave dreams?"

"Izzy," her father said, his tone soft but firm.

"I didn't mean," she stammered. "I mean–" Isabella couldn't figure out how to save this. She'd broken her promise to her father, and even though it was something so silly as this, she knew he'd be upset. Your word is your word, he'd say. With the heat beginning rise in her cheeks and tears leaking from the corner of her eyes, Isabella pushed back from the table and ran upstairs back into her room. She climbed into bed and pulled the covers over her head. She was mortified.

A few minutes later, she heard her door open, and footsteps shuffle across the carpet. First, they went over to her brother's crib, then they drew closer to her cocoon of blankets. Her father cleared his throat quietly and sat down on the edge of her bed. Isabella curled away from him, knowing that he would be disappointed because she'd broken her word. He always stressed that you shouldn't lie or break a promise.

"Izzy," he said quietly, "sweetie, I know you're still awake." Isabella tried not moving, hoping that her father would leave and not talk to her about it until the morning after he'd had a chance to sleep on it. Her mother had always told her that things seemed better after you sleep on them. She wasn't sure that she believed it, but she hoped it could be right this time. Her father just sat there in silence, waiting for her to respond. Before too long, she rolled over onto her back and looked up at him with a huff.

"What was that all about downstairs?" he asked, his voice already on edge. Isabella was angry at herself for breaking her promise and angry at him for leaving, but most of all, she was just upset that she still felt like she needed him to keep her nightmares away. She stared up at him through the darkness and fought to keep her tears from flowing.

"I'm sorry," she started, and the words just poured out of her, "I know that I promised, I didn't mean to tell mom, I just— She wanted to help, but she can't. She doesn't know how to, not like you. And it's not like you can do the whole weaving dreams thing away, so I don't know what it matters. I know you need to go, but I'm scared because the dreams keep getting worse when you're not home, and the nightmares are going to get bad again, then Mom's going to get mad at me because I'll keep waking Tucker up, and then waking her up, and I'm sorry." Isabella was almost out of breath by the time she finished and quietly added, "Please don't be mad at me." When she was done unloading her words, she wiped her eyes and lay looking up at her father, waiting for him to say something.

He rubbed the back of his neck with his right hand and sighed. "I know Izzy," he began, "but you shouldn't have broken your word."

She tried to cut in, but he held up his hand and raised his eyebrows to signal that he wasn't done talking yet. Izzy sighed and settled in for the lecture she was sure was coming.

"You shouldn't have broken your word," he began again, "because our word is one of the only things that we have full control over. The trust we earn from others is something precious to hold on to. Don't throw it away so lightly." Izzy had heard this lecture before about trust and lying, and she knew what was coming next. "But this time," her father continued, "I owe you an apology."

"What?" Izzy hadn't seen that coming.

"It's true," he said, patting her arm through the covers. "I'm sorry baby-girl, I should never have asked you to keep a secret from your mother. The trust between you and her, always telling your mother and me the truth, is more important than any promise, and I should never have put you in that position. I'm sorry."

Isabella felt a flood of relief and sat up to hug her father, his scruffy beard catching on her hair and pulling it in her face. "Thank you, Dad," she said, squeezing him again before she lay back on her pillow.

"It's alright."

"But now Mom knows," Izzy wasn't sure why he had needed it to be kept a secret, but she was sure he had his reasons. "Is that going to get you in trouble?"

He chuckled, "No, sweetie, honestly, your mother doesn't believe the whole dream weaving thing either. Don't give me that look. I know you don't buy it. Most people, when they grow up, stop believing in things like that. Too much like magic for them."

"It is kinda weird," she said.

"So am I baby-girl," he leaned in and kissed her on the forehead before sitting back up and rubbing his hands together. "Now, what do you say we make you a whopper of a dream to last while I'm away for work? What do you say, humor me one more time?"

While listening to him describe a fantastical adventure where she was riding a horse with a golden coat and snow-white mane, she watched her father's hands weaving together slowly. As he did this, the darkness in the room seemed to recede, and it almost looked like strings of light danced around his hands. When he was done, Isabella had an epic dream woven for her, and after implanting it in her head, her father kissed her good night, walked over to check on Tucker, who was still sleeping peacefully, and left the room.

Isabella lay there for a little while thinking about what her father had told her and her mother's reaction. She felt terrible. Her father had always told the craziest stories, but eventually, all stories lose their magic. She knew her father just wanted to keep her a little kid forever with the stories and the nicknames, and part of her loved that about him. After a while, her eyelids pulled shut, and she found herself standing on the edge of a field of rainbow flowers, next to her was a tall horse with a golden coat. She rubbed it's neck and smiled as it whinnied and curled it's large head around her as if giving her a comforting hug.

❧ THREE ❧

I sabella woke up to the soft warmth of her bed. She always liked a lot of blankets because their weight made her feel safe. She never really minded the heat, but tonight, she was sweating and must have thrown some of her blankets off earlier. The sun was still not up, but the light of the moon gave her enough to see the familiar outlines of her bedroom. She lay there, happy in the peaceful silence. Her lamp and dresser stood over by the window, and Tucker's crib, a new addition to her room which she was not happy about, tucked against the opposite wall.

She rolled toward the wall and pulled the covers back over herself. The room was quieter than it had been since Tucker had moved in with her while his room was being fixed. Between his sound machine, which thankfully turned off after a little while, and his breathing, which begrudgingly she was beginning to find comforting, a fact she would never admit to her parents. She lay there now and tried to listen for his soft snoring. She could almost feel the silence in the room, the weight of the blankets pulling her back to sleep. She listened harder for her brother's snoring, but couldn't hear anything. Rolling back over, Isabella stared at the crib, trying to make out the shape of her sleeping brother, but all she could see was his stuffed, corduroy lion hanging half out between the slats of the crib.

Tucker never went anywhere without that stupid corduroy lion, but maybe her mother had brought him out to be changed. She couldn't remember that ever happening, but that didn't mean it wasn't something that could happen. Her father had left for his work trip that morning, so maybe her mother had just brought Tucker into bed with her to get some more sleep. Isabella rolled back over and tried to go back to sleep, but something kept nagging at the back of her mind. Something felt wrong about her room, but she couldn't place it. With an annoyed sigh, Isabella threw back her covers and found her slippers at the edge of her bed where she left them. Wiping sleep from her eyes, she shuffled over to her brother's crib and saw that the blankets were strewn around the floor in front of the crib. She'd never seen either of her parents leave the blankets like that, typically they were draped over the edge of the crib. Without thinking about it, Isabella draped the blankets over the edge of the crib and grabbed Leo. She shuffled out of her room and down the hall toward Tucker's room.

The lights were off, and she went in anyway assuming her mother just hadn't turned them on, but it was empty and still had the plywood her father had put over the broken window. Isabella was beginning to get nervous. She walked back into the hall wishing that her father was home.

"Mom?" she called out. "Mom, where are you?" She called out walking to the door of her parent's room.

The door was open slightly, so she pushed her way in. The curtains were pulled back and a light summer breeze caught their edge billowing them. "Mom?" she said walking closer to the bed. The covers were bunched up toward the middle of the bed, and both pillows looking slept on. She wondered if her father had changed his mind and come back from the airport after she'd fallen asleep. "Dad?"

Isabella pulled at the sleeve of her nightgown and looked around the dark room. There was no answer to her calls, and all of the rooms upstairs seemed to be empty. She knew that her parents didn't like her to come downstairs when she was supposed to be in bed, but she was beginning to get nervous. "Mom?" she called from the top of the stairs. She heard something banging against a door downstairs, looking back at her open bedroom door, she considered climbing back into her bed, pulling the covers over her head, and hoping she fell back asleep. Instead, Isabella bit her bottom lip and started down the stairs. Something wasn't right, and she needed to figure it out.

As she neared the bottom of the stairs, she heard the banging again from the kitchen. She thought that her mother could have been in the kitchen, getting a late-night snack, people did that, she thought.

"Mom," she said, quieter now, "Dad?" More banging answered her, this time it seemed to become more fervent when she called out. Muffled voices were coming from the kitchen, it sounded like her parents, but there was something wrong with the sound. The only light in the room came from the one window over the sink and the glaring microwave clock reading 2:07 AM. "Hello?" she called rounding the corner into the room.

The banging sound and the voices were both coming from the basement door. She could hear her mother and father's voices clearly behind the door, intermixed with them was a whimpering cry from Tucker. Isabella rushed to the door, trying the handle as the muffled voices of her parents called frantically behind the door.

"Dad, Mom, what's going on?"

"Izzy, thank God you're alright," her father's voice sounded worried. "Listen, sweetie, you need to get out of the house right now."

"It's two in the morning," she pressed her ear to the door, "I'm in my nightgown."

"Listen, sweetheart," his voice shook like it was on the edge of tears, something she'd never heard in her father's voice before, "you need to leave now, get to the back door and get out of here."

"Hold on," she said trying the doorknob again, "I think the door is locked. Can you unlock it from in there? It sounds like you're telling me to go outside."

"Yes Izzy," her mother's voice had tears in it, "go outside now."

"Let me get the keys," she said looking around the kitchen, "you put them in the junk drawer, right?"

"Just go," her father called through the door.

Isabella went across the kitchen, confused about why her parents kept telling her to leave. The key was somewhere in the junk drawer. She knew that once she got them out, they could explain everything that was going on. She opened the drawer and started shuffling through papers, half-used rolls of tape, and knickknacks that they kept in the drawer. It was hard to see, but she didn't want to turn on the light.

Another bang, louder than the ones from her parents behind the door came from the other room. It sounded as if someone had bumped into a table. She froze, her hands around a used battery that she just realized wasn't the small flashlight on the keychain. She looked toward the dark rectangle of the kitchen door, dimly outlined by the white molding in the moonlight. She listened to her parents' muffled cries from behind the basement door and another bang came from the other room, followed by the scuff of something being moved along the floor.

Isabella realized why her parents had been telling her to leave, but the only way out now was either through that doorway or out of the basement hatch. Her search for the basement key intensified. Now it was more about getting out with her parents instead of getting her parents out. She heard their calls to her become more frantic as she pulled the drawer out of the cabinet and spilled the contents on the kitchen table. Another bump from the front room made her jump, a small gasp escaping from her quivering lips.

She spread her hands through the junk that littered the table, but the key wasn't there. Isabella knew this was where they kept it, her father had a habit of accidentally locking himself down there at least twice a year, and she was often the one to help him out. She knew the key was here, but it wasn't. She searched through the pile again, then went over to the door, tears welling up in her eyes.

"I can't find the key," she cried, her ear against the door, "I'm so sorry Daddy, it's just not there."

"It's okay baby girl," his voice was soft, soothing almost, "don't worry about it, just go to the living room and get out through the front door. We'll be alright."

"I'll get you out," she said, her tears flowing down her cheeks, "the shed. I'll get the key to the padlock for the hatchway. Meet me over there, okay?"

"Alright sweetie," his voice sounded sad, "just get to the front door, and get outside. Don't let it see you."

"Dad?"

"Go, now," his voice was insistent. "We love you, Izzy, get out safely."

Another scuffing sound from the other room made her jump again. Her legs felt weak, and her fingers shook as they played with her sleeve. A sob hitched in the throat as she pushed away from the door, "I'm sorry," she said, "I'm so sorry. I love you."

As she looked away from the door, preparing to make a break for the living room, a large shadow blocked the moonlight from the other room. Isabella gasped and backed away from the door into the kitchen counter. She reached her hand back, grabbing an apple that was sitting in a bowl, and threw it at the shadow. The apple passed through it and bounded off the wall behind it with a thud. She tensed as the shadow moved into the room, first going to the table, then heading toward the basement door.

Isabella rounded the other side of the table and broke for the now empty doorway to the hall. She heard a loud bang against the basement door, the sound of wood splintering. She paused in the doorway, if she left now, she'd make it to the front door while this thing was distracted with her parents, but what would that mean for them? Taking another deep breath, she turned around and looked at the looming shadow bashing into the basement door.

"Hey," she called out before she thought it through. "You forgot something."

For a second there was no response, but then the shadow shifted and began to slide toward her eclipsing the light from the microwave clock as it moved through the kitchen. Isabella didn't move at first; she hadn't fully thought her actions through, but now that the attention was on her, her parents would be safe for the time being. She felt the cold fear flowing off of the shadow and realized that she still hadn't moved. Taking a stumbling step backward, she turned and ran through the dark hall into the living room, jumping over a lamp that had been knocked to the floor, and headed for the front door.

She let out a grunt as she slammed into the door. Fumbling with the lock, she looked over her shoulder as the shadow emerged from the hall, moving slowly but steadily through the room. The lamp shattered as the shadow passed, and Isabella, just getting the door unlocked, threw the door open and turned to look right into the eyes of an enormous white wolf.

The wolf stood with its four lean legs spread out, it's shoulders and neck hunched and tense. The fur on its sides quivered as it let out a low, guttural growl. Isabella had never seen something look both so beautiful and so terrifying in her life and stood frozen as the wolf's lips drew back into a snarl, showing long white fangs glittering in the moonlight. Lowering its body and whipping its tail once, the wolf leaped toward her in one efficient and deadly strike.

Sitting up, Isabella looked around her and tried to catch her breath. She was disoriented and tried to get her bearings in the dark room. She was sweating and shaking as her eyes adjusted to the darkness around her. Soon the moonlight was bright enough to see the familiar outlines of her bedroom. She lay there, taking long shaky breaths. Her lamp and dresser stood over by the window.

A whimpering noise came from the crib on the opposite side of her room, and Isabella let out a shaky breath that boarded on a cry. Tucker shifted in his sleep, kicking his legs and whimpering again before he cried out and woke himself up. For a moment there was only the sound of their ragged breathing in the room, then Tucker let out a terrified cry. Isabella heard a shuffling from across the hallway, and eventually, the door to her room opened letting light from the hallway and the silhouette of her mother into her room.

"Oh Tucker," Izzy's mother sighed groggily as she walked toward his crib, "it is too early for you to get up. Lay back down buddy." She looked over at Isabella sitting up on her elbow watching her mother with relieved intensity. "Sweetheart, did he wake you up too. I'm sorry, this has to be hard for you. Think you'll be able to get back to sleep?"

"Yeah, sure, goodnight." Izzy wasn't sure she was telling the truth, but she rolled over and pulled the covers up over her head and stared at the wall. By the time her mother had gotten Tucker back to sleep and given Izzy a goodnight kiss, she was almost positive that sleep was not going to be happening again tonight.

FOUR

Isabella had fallen back to sleep and woke up from a dream she didn't remember, disoriented again. There was a sound she couldn't quite place, repetitive and loud. Her first thought was the smoke detectors, but those would say fire, this was wordless noise. She rubbed her sleep encrusted eyes and looked around again. Across the room, Tucker was standing in the corner of his crib, bouncing up and down, calling Daddy. Isabella pulled the covers over her head the grunted.

Not long after she'd woken up, her mother shuffled back into the room and went right over to Tucker's crib. "Tucker, buddy, you need to go back to sleep," her voice was strained. "I can't do these late nights all the time."

Tucker's cried ramped up when she picked him up. "Daddy, Daddy, I want Daddy."

"Your daddy isn't here right now," she said, "I'm going to have to be good enough." Her voice had the sound she gets when Izzy has done something she should have known not to do.

"I want Daddy," he was upset, but that was making her mother worse.

"I told you he's not here," she scolded him, "so, do we sit down and rock, or are you going back in your crib?"

"Outside," he declared.

One look out the window showed Izzy that any outdoor trip would need to wait. Forget that it had been raining for the past two days, the sun wasn't even up.

"No," her mother said, "you are not going outside."

Isabella chucked at Tucker's pout filled "Why not?" She could almost see him standing there with his arms crossed.

"Tucker," her mother's voice was short and angry, "you are not going outside. Lay yourself down, or I am walking out of this room and going back to bed."

He started crying again, and Isabella knew this was going to be a long night. Between the shadow figure in her nightmare and her brother's meltdown, she was positive that sleep was done for the night.

After what felt like forever, Tucker fell into a whimpering sleep and Isabella's mother came over and sat on the side on her bed. She silently stroked her daughter's hair and hummed a quiet song. Isabella felt the tug of sleep begin to pull her into her dreams. When her mother stopped and bent down to kiss the back of her head, Isabella smiled and pulled the covers up to her neck.

"Sleep well my little angel," her mother said, then the springs in the bed creaked as she stood up. "Let's hope that's the last time. I'm not sure how much more I can take." With a sigh, she left the room, closing the door slowly so the latch didn't wake Tucker.

Isabella rolled over and looked at the crib. She felt sorry for her mother and hated that her father wasn't here to help with Tucker. She thought of her own nightmares and shivered despite the heavy blankets. Her father's dream to take her through the week hadn't even lasted the first night and a half, but it had been a good dream. She thought about riding the horse again and sighed.

Across the room, she heard her brother kicking his legs and whimpering, clearly in another nightmare. She felt bad for him, but it wasn't fair that she didn't get to sleep anymore because his room had problems. She understood why her parents didn't have him in their room, her father had been so cranky when the crib was in there. He said that he never got more than a half-hour sleep because he'd be up with every noise. She liked her rested father better and her rested mother. They were more patient and understanding when they could get sleep. The whimpering from across the room grew louder and Isabella rolled her eyes. She knew that in a few minutes, Tucker would be awake again and yelling, then her mother would come in blurry-eyed and annoyed, and tomorrow would be difficult for all of them.

She pushed the covers off of her and threw her bathrobe over her shoulders. Walking over to Tucker's crib, she watched him as he stirred restlessly in his sleep. He wasn't going to be out much longer, she'd seen this process at least ten times since his crib had been moved into her room. She brought the stool she used to get to the top shelf of her closet over to his crib and waited patiently for her little brother to wake with screams from his nightmare. His blond hair was matted down with sweat, and he'd kicked his covers off. She looked around for Leo, his corduroy stuffed lion, and found it pushed between the slats of the crib. She shivered slightly remembering her own nightmare. She didn't have time to dwell on it though because thankfully, that was the moment that Tucker began to cry out.

Isabella reached into his crib before he could stand up and began rubbing his back, much like her parents had always done to soothe her. When his cries continued to amp up, she started to sing the only lullaby she could remember, the one her mother used to sing her as she rocked her to sleep.

"Too ra loo ra loo la, too ra loo ra lai–" she continued to sing as the door to her room opened up and her mother, looking exhausted, stood there, her hand on her heart and smiled. Isabella smiled back and nodded at her before turning back to Tucker and continuing her song. She heard the door close and continued singing as his cries became soft whimpers and those faded into the soft snores he has on his good nights. "–Hush not don't you cry. Too ra loo ra loo la, too ra loo ra lai. Too ra loo ra loo ra, it's an Irish lullaby."

Isabella continued to hum the song softly as she climbed back into her bed and pulled the covers up over her shoulders. The comforting weight of her blankets hugged her, and she smiled to herself. It felt good to help her mother when she could.

Tucker snored peacefully behind her, and she felt pride swell up as sleep claimed her.

Isabella found herself in an empty field, surrounded by green grass and wildflowers. The breeze smelled like a spring rain had just passed, and she ran her hand across some of the wet flowers. The tall grass to her left moved as something glided through the grass headed toward a stream trickling nearby. She listened to the birds singing as they flew through the clear blue sky. She ran through the grass, her bare feet kicking up the water droplets on the grass, heading toward the steady sound of joyful laughter over by the stream.

"Hello?" She searched the grass for where the laughter is coming from, but as she stood on the edge of the stream, the laughter was replaced by the trickling of water.

Across the stream, a small red fox lapped up the water. Isabella watched it drink, but as she moved to step across the stream, the fox noticed her movement and skittered away into the long grass.

"Don't go," she called after it, but the fox had disappeared.

"He'll be back," a deep voice sounded from the grass across the stream. With the voice, a cool breeze picks up, causing Isabella to shiver and pull her bathrobe tightly around herself.

"Hello?" She searches the front of the grass but couldn't see where the voice came from. The voice was vaguely familiar, but she couldn't place it. "Do I know you?"

"No," the voice says, it is an emotionless voice, tinged with danger, but it didn't scare her. "I am a friend."

"If I don't—" Isabella's question died on her lips as a large wolf, standing almost as tall as she did, rose from the grass on the other side of the stream and walked from the cover of the flowers.

"Don't be afraid," the wolf said as it stalked toward the edge of the water. The night-black fir around its muzzle stood in stark contrast to the lustrous white that graced the rest of its sleek form.

Isabella took a step backward toward the grass on her side of the stream. She'd read about wolves in one of her father's books before and knew that there was no way she could outrun it, but she wasn't going to stand there and be eaten. The muscles in the wolf's shoulders tensed as he watched Isabella back up.

"I need to give you a message, girl," the wolf's deep voice silenced the birds and sent shivers down Isabella's spine, "I do not wish to chase you."

"A message?"

"You must find your way."

"Find my way where?" Despite the unnerving chill the wolf's voice sent through her, Isabella stood her ground and looked the enormous beast in the eye. His bulk softened, and he sat across from her, his head tilting slightly from the side.

"You will not travel alone when you go, remember that. There is someone here who waits for you."

"Where am I supposed to be going?"

"You must always remember that you are in control. Fear is only an illusion of your mind. There is power with you, but it is wild, untested, shifting like a scent in the breeze."

"I don't understand what you are saying," she said. "Not to mention that I'm talking to a wolf."

"You will understand in time, but you need to be patient." With that, the wolf stood up and turned to slink back into the grass.

"Wait," Isabella called out, but as the wolf turned around and settled its black eyes on her she forgot the question she was going to ask and instead stammered out, "Do you have a name?"

"Yes," the wolf seemed to consider something, tilting its head to the side, but didn't say anything further.

"Well?"

"I will see you again," the wolf responded, then tensing its haunches, bounded off into the flowers. Isabella watched the grass sway as it went until she couldn't tell the difference between the wind and the passing of the wolf.

When the wolf was out of sight, the birds resumed their songs, and the stream, which seemed to have silenced during their conversation, sounded too loud. Isabella turned and walked back toward a white canopy billowing in the distance. The wolf's ominous warning about seeing her again still rang in her ears, but for some reason, she felt safe, at least for now, and the billowing white cloth of the canopy was a curiosity she just couldn't pass up.

In the darkened room, the sound of peaceful breathing permeated the night air. Isabella, eyes moving quickly beneath closed lids, shifted slightly in her sleep, and laughed. Across the room, Tucker snores soundly tucked away in his crib, Leo held tightly in his arm. The air seems to buzz with peaceful energy and for the briefest moment, a faint blue thread of light flared from under Isabella's blankets and then faded. The two siblings slept peacefully until late in the morning when the sun, having recently burned off the morning haze, shone through a slit in the curtain, and falling on Tucker's face, woke him from some happy dream.

FIVE

"Izzy," her mother called from the kitchen, "could you get your brother and play with him."

"But Mom, I'm doing something."

"So am I," her voice was tense, "and if you want to eat dinner tonight, I need to be able to keep doing it."

Isabella rolled her eyes, closed the cover of her iPad, and got up from the chair she had draped herself across. She knew better than to argue with her mother when she had that tone in her voice. Placing her iPad down on the side table, she went into the kitchen.

"Come on Tucker," the halfheartedness dripping from her voice, "let's go play trains or something."

"Play trains with me?" Tucker asked with a smile that split his face.

"Thank you, sweetie," her mother said smiling at her, "he was just completely underfoot. I thought I was going to step on him or toss him in the oven by mistake." She laughed half-heartedly at her own joke.

"It's alright," Isabella said. "What time is dinner?"

"Probably a half-hour," she said, "but remember, no screen time after dinner."

"But Mom," she protested, "you made me stop to play with Tucker. That's not fair."

"Maybe not, but it's what's happening," she said. "Your dad isn't here to occupy him while I'm cooking, so I need your help."

Isabella crossed her arms and glared at her mother's back. Not fair, she said under her breath.

"I appreciate it, Izzy," she added, almost like an afterthought.

"Iee-iee," Tucker still couldn't get her name right, "look! Choo-choo train!"

Isabella looked over to see Tucker standing on the chair with her iPad held in his hand moving it back and forth across the back of the chair.

"Tucker," she cried rushing over to the back of the chair to grab the iPad from his hand, "don't do that, you're going to break it."

"Mommy," Tucker cried, "Iee-iee's mean."

"Izzy," her mother scolded, "play nice."

"But mom—"

"I said play nice, I can't stop every two seconds to keep you from fighting. Just keep him occupied until dinner's ready."

"He had my iPad."

"You shouldn't have left it where he can get it."

"If it was in my hands then he wouldn't have gotten it either," Isabella said under her breath.

"Izzy," her mother's voice was warning enough, clearly she hadn't been quiet enough with her last answer.

For the rest of the night, Isabella kept her brother busy. She was old enough to know when she pushed her luck too far by talking back, and she didn't want her mother to take away the iPad for the rest of the weekend. She was always more on edge when Izzy's father wasn't home, and when she was on edge, Izzy knew she was far more likely to get in trouble. So she did what she could to fly under the radar.

Instead of playing her games on her the iPad, she spent the next half hour pushing a little wooden train around some tracks on the floor. That was when Tucker wasn't taking it from her hand or telling her she was doing it wrong. After dinner, the three of them played Candy Land and Shoots and Ladders.

"But he's cheating," Isabella had protested when Tucker moved his piece up the ladder during her turn. "You never let me play like that."

"We did," her mother said with placating patience. "He's two, just let him have his fun?"

"What about my fun?"

"We can play around him," she'd suggested. The idea worked too until Tucker noticed and started grabbing their pieces too.

"I'm just going upstairs to read," Isabella said throwing her playing piece in the box. "You two can play his way."

"Me too coming," Tucker said.

"No."

"Tucker, honey," her mother said, trying to get his attention. "Let Izzy have some quiet time." She kept talking to him, probably getting him to focus on something else for a few moments while Isabella escaped upstairs. It must have worked, because, by the time they came up, Izzy had finished her book and was looking through her shelves for a new one.

"Feeling any better sweetie?" her mother asked when she brought Tucker up for bed.

"A little bit," she said picking a new book from her shelf. "I was going to read a little more before bed."

"The light will keep him up," her mother said, "besides, we have a busy day tomorrow. Why don't you get some sleep."

"But mom," Isabella glared at her mother, "that's not fair. It's way too early for me to go to bed. I'm not a baby."

Her mother just kissed the top of her head and said, "Why don't you read a little downstairs while I get your brother ready," Isabella looked up at her and smiled. "Just make sure you're quiet as a mouse when you come back in, you know how light a sleeper your little brother is."

"Okay," Isabella kissed her mother on the cheek before she grabbed her book and raced downstairs to her favorite reading spot, the overstuffed papasan chair jammed into the corner of her father's home office. She curled up in the chair like a cat and pulled a blanket over her. This– this was relaxation she thought to herself as she opened her book and began reading. After a couple of chapters, her mother came down from putting Tucker to bed and shooed her upstairs. By then she'd read the same sentence about three times, so she didn't bother arguing.

After getting ready, she snuck into her bedroom and closed the door behind her. The latch on the door clanked loudly in the silent room, and her brother stirred in his crib. She froze in the middle of her room, knowing that her mother would kill her if he woke. She listened as he shifted in his crib and settled back to sleep. Letting out the breath she didn't realize she was holding, Isabella climbed into her bed and, pulling the covers over her, rolled to the wall and closed her eyes.

"Izzy," her mother's voice woke her up, "you woke him up."

"No, I didn't. I was almost asleep."

"Well, I don't know," her mother said, "you just came in here, and now he's crying."

Isabella noticed that he was crying, but she hadn't heard him before. She must have fallen asleep within seconds of laying down, but she still didn't think it was her fault he'd woken up.

"I was laying here."

"Okay," her mother said, ending the argument. "Just help make sure he stays down tonight. I need to get some sleep, last night was brutal."

She soothed and cooed to him until he was quiet, then she left the room, making sure not to latch the door. Isabella rolled on her back, folded her arms over her head, and exhaled. She didn't like having to help with her brother. He'd been a mistake anyway. Her parents had said they didn't intend to have another kid after her, but then they did, and now she needed to share her room because of stupid branch smashing through his window. None of this was fair.

After a little while of staring at the ceiling, she heard Tucker whimper and kick his feet. Isabella knew that it was only a matter of time before he woke up again. She silently wished her father was there, he could stop anyone from having bad dreams, give them good ones too, and as much as she missed it for herself, she was beginning to miss it for her brother's sake too. Then she could get some proper sleep.

When he cried this time, she went over to his crib to calm him down so her mother didn't have to. Looking down at her brother's tear-streaked cheeks, she felt bad for him. He was so scared that his little body was shaking.

"Bad dream buddy?" she asked hugging him over the edge of the crib.

"Yes," his bottom lip quivered as he fought to control his tears.

"What was your dream?"

"Spooky," he said, "room was spooky."

"Poor little man," she said, then she laughed to herself about how much like her father she sounded when talking to him like this. She'd seen him talking to Tucker like this countless times, then she got an idea. "Want me to get rid of it?"

"Uh-huh," he nodded solemnly.

"Okay buddy," she smiled, "I've seen Daddy do this, let's see if it works for you." She thought about what sort of dream would be good for her brother, then settled on what she would like. "You're in a field of wildflowers, there is a little stream flowing through the middle of it, and a bunch of birds singing and little gardener snakes, you know the kind that you like finding in the woodpile?"

Tucker nodded, smiling as he wiped away his tears.

Isabella started twisting her fingers together like she'd seen her father do. "Right, so you're there, and your friends, and you're all playing trains."

"Choo-choo train?"

"Yup buddy, lots of choo-choo trains. Tons of them," she tapped her finger to her lips before she wove her fingers together again. "So you are playing trains in this field and there are lots of little animals."

"Leo," he held his stuffed lion.

"Of course, Leo is there too. Running around in the field," she felt a lightness in her head as she tried to focus on weaving her brother a great dream. "And you're all running around and having a blast. Sound good??

"Dream," he said bouncing in his crib, his previous nightmare forgotten.

"Okay, and you're wandering in the field and you're not going to get up," she said trying to see if she could get his to sleep for the rest of the night. "You're wandering in this field and you don't want to leave it, it's too much fun."

She cupped her hands next to her brother's temple, like she'd seen her father do, and blew through them. She felt a faint shock when she touched her brother and jumped. "Okay, now you need to lay down if you're going to have that great dream sister made for you."

"Thank you Iee-iee," he said drowsily and lay down. She pulled the covers over him and lay down in her bed.

She lay on her back and listened until Tucker's breathing evened out. He whimpered a couple of times, called her sleepily once, then she heard him sigh softly and begin to snore. Isabella rolled over toward the wall. "Let's hope this works," she said to herself. If this worked, she thought, she would be a hit at the next sleepover.

SIX

The sun was bright through the crack in the curtains when Isabella woke up the next morning. She first looked over to Tucker's crib, noticed it was empty, and once again Leo was jammed between the slats. Her mind flashed to her nightmare the other night, but it had been dark then, and darkness always makes things seem worse than they are. Though, knowing Tucker, he'd want that lion when he realized he didn't have it. Isabella appreciated her mother getting him quickly and letting her sleep, which explains why she forgot the lion. She reminded herself to help her mother today as a thank you; it's easy to forget the nice things people do for you sometimes.

Yawning, Isabella walked down the stairs straightening her t-shirt. Her mother was in the kitchen and the smell of pancakes and sausages wafted up the stairs. She walked into the kitchen, Leo in hand, and kissed her mother on the cheek.

"Thanks, Mom," she said as she looked around the silent kitchen and living room.

"It's been so peaceful this morning," her mother said taking the pancakes off the griddle and replacing them with fresh batter. "I know your father usually makes pancakes on Sundays, so I figured since you were still sleeping– I made sausages too," she smiled over the spatula, "I keep trying to get your father to make some, but you know how he is." She laughed. Isabella had always loved her mother's laugh, it was bright and lilting and had the quality of a bird in the springtime. Unfortunately, she rarely got to hear her mother's laugh.

"It smells really good."

"Oh good," she looked at the stack of pancakes on the counter, "but I think I made too much, what do you think?"

"I think you were planning on inviting Tucker's whole daycare over, who's going to eat all of that."

"I know," her mother laughed again and Isabella bathed in the sound. She always thought her own laugh sounded forced and jagged, but her mother's was sheer music. "Can you set the table then go get your brother?"

"Sure, where is he?"

"What do you mean where is he?" She picked up her coffee from the counter and took a tentative sip of the steaming caramel-colored liquid inside. "I'd assume he's still in your room asleep."

"I thought you brought him down here." Isabella looked at Leo who she'd set on the counter, "I brought Leo down for him."

"Oh, you better get Leo back up there," she said smiling over her mug, "he's going to be mad when he wakes up and that silly lion isn't there."

"Mom," Isabella furrowed her brow, "his crib is empty."

"Izzy, come on, don't be difficult."

"Mom," she looked at her mother trying to make her understand the horror that was settling in the pit of her stomach. "Tucker is not in his crib. Are you sure you didn't bring him down here?"

"What do you mean, am I sure, where else would he be?"

"Can he climb out?"

"Izzy, this isn't funny," her mother's face paled as she fought to ignore what Isabella was saying. "Go get your brother and– Izzy?"

"Mom," Isabella felt the tears burning the back of her eyes, "you brought him downstairs, didn't you?"

Her mother set her coffee cup on the edge of the counter and rushed upstairs. Isabella walked over to push it over more so it didn't get knocked off, but as she approached the cup, her mother let out a heartrending cry from upstairs, the suddenness of the panic in her voice as she called Tucker made Isabella jump and knock the porcelain mug to the floor. Time slowed down as the mug toppled from her hands, spilling the hot caramel liquid into the air, her mother's footsteps thudding down the stairs as she called her son's name, the splash of the coffee hitting the floor hidden by the choking sound in her mother's voice. Isabella stood an incomprehensible pillar in the storm, the shattering of the porcelain mug on the tile floor shocked the world back to full speed as her mother rushed around the corner and caught Isabella in her arms, wet tears sticking her hair to her mother's cheeks.

"Izzy," her mother's voice was fringed with panic, "Izzy, sweetie, where is your brother?" She pulled back, Isabella's hair stretched between them until her mother smoothed it out with one hand. "Where's Tucker?"

"Mom?" She knew something wasn't right, her mother had brought Tucker downstairs, he must be playing with his trains in the living room. "Mommy, he's not down here?"

"No sweetie," she said looking into the tears welling in her daughter's eyes, "I didn't bring him down here. Are you sure you didn't hear anything last night?"

"No," Isabella was sure she would have noticed someone coming into the room.

"Did anything happen?"

"I—" Isabella thought about the dream she'd woven for her brother like her father had done, and a pang of guilt shot through her.

"Yes, sweetie?" Her mother's expectant eyes shone in the morning light from the kitchen window.

"I – I was asleep," she looked down at the floor, her shoulders hitched as she fought the tears welling up in her eyes, and her mother pulled her into an embrace and squeezed her tightly as she shook beneath her tears.

"It's okay honey," she kept repeating. "We'll find him," a claim that sounded more like it was to calm her mother than to help Isabella.

The smell of smoke preceded the smoke detectors by a few seconds. The blaring seemed to snap her mother into action, she swore under her breath and fumbled with the knobs on the stove. Then, grabbing a potholder for the counter, she threw the griddle and smoking pancakes into the sink and turned on the water. Steam filled the kitchen, causing the light from the kitchen window to take on an eery ethereal quality.

The next few hours were a blur of activity. After searching the house, emptying closets, and crawling under beds where Tucker liked to hide when they would play hide and seek, Isabella and her mother searched the yard, hoping that he had somehow wandered outside without neither of them noticed. When all the searches came up empty, Isabella's mother got in the car to search the neighborhood and the park down the street where they would go on nice days and Tucker would ride the twisty slide for hours. Isabella was left home so someone would be there in case he showed up, so she cleaned the spilled coffee and swept the shards of the mug as best she could before sitting down to cold pancakes and sausage, which she ate mechanically, not tasting the sweet maple syrup she loved so much. When she was done, she found herself on the steps looking into the living room at her brother's wooden train track, hugging Leo as her tears wet the top of the corduroy lion's mane. Her mother, now home after finding nothing, spent the rest of the time on the phone. First the police, then several tearful calls to her father's voicemail, with frantic, hopeful calls to the neighbors and family in between. Eventually, the police came, searched the house, asked their questions, and left promising to check back in if they found anything. One officer, probably his first or second year out of school, offered to stay, but her mother sent him on his way with a distracted wave and went back to dialing her father's number. She'd stopped leaving messages but was calling him nonstop.

Isabella got up from the stairs, set Leo in her mother's lap, and went into the kitchen. She made her mother a peanut butter and jelly sandwich, poured her some milk, and brought both to her, setting it on the table beside the couch.

"Mom," she said tentatively, crouching down to look into her mother's eyes. The empty look in them scared her. She knew that her mother got sad sometimes, sometimes really sad, and she was sure this would be one of those times. Isabella took a deep breath, squared her shoulders, and taking the phone from her mother's hands, sat down beside her. "Mom, you need to eat something, it's almost two o'clock."

"I'm not hungry, baby."

"I know," she said, pointing to the plate and glass on the table next to her, "but you need to eat anyway. You haven't had anything all day, and you always tell me that you can't solve a problem on an empty stomach."

"Oh baby," she pulled Isabella into her, her voice hitching, "I'm so glad you're here. I don't know what I would do without you."

"Don't worry Mom," another pang of guild course up Isabella's spine, "we'll find him. I made you a sandwich, eat now. I'm going to make myself one too."

"You have this one," her mother insisted, "I'll make one for myself."

"No, you eat. I have this." Isabella patted her mother's knee as she got up and made herself a sandwich.

Isabella's father didn't call them back until dinner time, and he didn't have good news. He hadn't gotten their messages because he had forgotten his phone at the hotel and was in meetings all day. Now, there was a problem with his plane, and they had to reschedule his flight. He'd be heading home on a red-eye and wouldn't be back at the house until the next morning at the earliest. Her mother cried a lot, and Isabella found herself sitting next to her, rubbing her hand in small circles on her mother's back like she'd done when Isabella would get sick. By the time night rolled around, they were both so worried that they skipped dinner, hoping that when Isabella's father came home he would somehow make everything better.

"You don't have to sleep in here." Isabella was surprised when her mother walked into her room carrying her pillow and a blanket and tossed both on the floor.

"I don't want you to have to be alone tonight," she'd said.

"I'll be okay, you checked the doors and the windows like seven times before we came upstairs." She motioned to the camera her parents had mounted on the wall when they moved Tucker into her room, "Plus, there's the baby monitor."

"Didn't do much good last night."

Isabella didn't know what to say to that. She didn't particularly mind having company tonight, but she wanted her mother to get a good night's sleep, and sleeping on her floor wouldn't do that. "Then take my bed, I'll sleep on the floor."

"No Izzy," she tucked Isabella in and sat on the edge of the bed, "I want to be here, I need to, in case– " she didn't need to finish her sentence, they both knew. "Just sleep well baby, I'll be with you all night, and Daddy will be home tomorrow. We'll figure this out."

Isabella rolled over and her mother rubbed her back, singing softly. Isabella listened to her mother's broken voice and felt her warm tears stream down her cheeks, dampening her pillow.

"Over in Killarney

Many years ago,

Me Mither sang a song to me

In tones so sweet and low. –"

As her mother sang the same song she had sung to her when Isabella was a baby, the old comfort caused all the fear that had welled in her throughout the day burst through to the surface, and with the last "Too-ra-loo-ra-loo-ral," her tears spent, exhaustion took her into a fitful sleep.

Isabella found herself standing in the middle of a frozen lake, the wind whipped across the surface, kicking up loose snow and ice into her face. She raised her arms to shield her eyes from the assaulting ice. She'd heard a howling in the distance, long and hollow-sounding against the roar of the wind.

"Hello?" she called out across the ice, only to have her voice echo back to her. "Hello," she called again, "is there anyone here?"

The hollow sound of a lone wolf's howl answered her, this time closer. Isabella looked around, unsure where the sound was coming from. Standing in the middle of the wind-swept ice, she felt a panic rising in her chest.

"Tucker," she called out, turning left and right, "Mom? Dad?" She could feel eyes on her through the raising storm that surrounded her. The sting of the ice hitting her unprotected skin increased her feelings of unease. Shivering, she scanned the ice-covered landscape for some shelter or some sign of life. Grabbing her shoulders in a futile attempt to keep her body warm, Isabella worried she was going to get hypothermia. The sound of crunching ice came clearly from behind her. Something was there, something big. Slowly, she turned and looked into the eyes of an arctic wolf. Its dark eyes even with her light blue ones. Her breath caught at the closeness of the white fangs against the black fur on the muzzle. She could feel the warm puffs from the wolf's breath. "You."

"Isabella," the wolf said, its voice the same mix of warmth and danger that she remembered from her other dream. "Go to him. He doesn't want to leave. He needs you."

"Who?" Though she knew who he was talking about, "Tucker."

"He needs your help," there was a low growl from the wolf as it looked back the way it had come. "Go now," the wolf bared its teeth to the wind, "they're coming for you both."

"Who's coming?"

"No time," the wolf turned his back on her, "go now."

With that the wolf let out a chilling howl and leaped, disappearing into the wind and snow.

Isabella sat up in bed drenched in sweat and shivering at the same time. The wolf's words echoed in her mind, *He doesn't want to leave.* Isabella thought back to the dream she'd given her brother the night before, she remembered telling him it was so fun he didn't want to leave, hoping that would keep him sleeping through the night. It was still late, and she knew that this was all her fault, but at least now she knew where he was and if her dad was telling the truth about this dream weaving stuff, she had an idea how to fix it and save her brother.

SEVEN

The moon shone brightly through her window, and her mother slept peacefully on the floor beside her bed. Isabella knew what she was about to do might make things worse for her mother in the short term, but Tucker would be back if she succeeded, and everything would be better again. Making her way around from the bathroom, she closed the door quietly and walked over to the window. The summer night was clear, and the crescent moon gave everything an ethereal light.

She was sure now where her brother was; the dream and that wolf had made it clear. What she had to do was think about her brother as she fell asleep, and she would dream about him. If this worked, there was a risk of getting lost in her dream, like her brother, but if there was a chance she could bring him back, she needed to try.

"I'm worried about him too, sweetie," her mother's groggy voice started her.

"I didn't mean to wake you."

"No, don't worry about it," her mother propped herself up on her elbow, using her free hand to rub the back of her neck. "My old bones weren't made to sleep on the floor."

"You're not old," Isabella went over to sit next to her mother on the floor, "the floor just isn't a good place to sleep. Why don't you go to bed? I'll be fine. I promise."

"You sure?"

"Get a good night's sleep," she got up and sat down on her bed again. "I'm going back to bed. I'll see you in the morning."

"Alright," her mother stood and gathered the blanket she'd brought, then she leaned down to kiss her Isabella and tuck her, "if you need anything, anything, come get me, alright?"

"I'll be good, Mom," Isabella smiled and pulled the covers tight under her chin, "don't worry."

"See you in the morning, honey," she paused at the door for a moment, "I love you."

"Love you too," Isabella said in a sleep heavy voice.

She heard her door close gently, the latch falling into place, and rolled back over onto her back, looked up at the glow in the dark stars her father had put on her ceiling, and hoped she was doing the right thing. She was pretty sure the wolf from her dream knew where her brother was. The wolf hadn't said given specifics, but he might as well have. She closed her eyes and sighed. Her friends would think she'd lost her mind, taking advice from wolves in her dreams.

"Okay," she said to the stars on her ceiling, "let's do this." She began to weave her fingers together and tried to describe the place she'd seen the wolf last. "I'm in the center of a snowstorm, standing in the middle of a frozen lake." She tried to remember everything she'd noticed, but it was a blank. Frozen lake and snow, great she thought to herself, what's the worst that can happen. She blew into her hands, spread them across her forehead, and closed her eyes, waiting for sleep to descend.

She stood in the middle of a snowstorm, on a frozen lake, and sighed.

"Here again," she told the wind. "Wolf? Hey, wolf? You here?" She heard the lonely howl and waited to see the black snout through the snow before she asked her question. "Is my brother here?"

"I have already told you he is not," there was an edge of annoyance in the wolf's voice.

"Right, but where is he?"

"He is where you put him. He is near the field with the trains and the steam. You will not find him here. It is not safe here."

"How do I get there?"

"The same way he did." The wolf turned to walk back the way it came.

Isabella called after it, "Wait, wolf, you're not going to help me?"

"It is not my place to help you."

"But you said I would have help?"

"And you will," the wolf bowed its head and closed its eyes, "just not me."

"Can I know your name? In case I need to call you again, so I don't have to call you wolf,"

The large wolf stopped, almost invisible in the swirling snow and ice, tilted its head to look over its shoulder, and nodded. "I can see no harm in you knowing, but I won't always be able to come. My journey lies with another. You can call me Vígolfr. But remember, I may not be able to come, so find my sister. She will help you." The powerful wolf sprang into the swirling storm and disappeared from view.

"Thanks," Isabella called after the wolf, "like that's easy to pronounce."

Sitting up sharply in bed for the fourth time that night, Isabella shivered despite the sweat coating her skin. She got up to open the window, letting the warm night air inside to clear her head. The crib sat along the wall opposite her bed, empty of the snoring, crying, train obsessed brother of hers, and tears formed in the corners of her eyes. She held her fists down by her sides and took a deep, shaking breath through clenched teeth.

Three times now, she tried to get to her brother, but no matter what she tried, she couldn't end up anywhere other than the middle of the frozen lake. Each time she had called for Vígolfr, or at least she'd tried, never quite sure she was pronouncing his name right, but he hadn't come since the first time. She had even tried calling his sister, not that she knew her name, but she hadn't come either. At this point, the sun was beginning to rise, and Isabella knew she would not have many more chances tonight.

"One more time," she said to herself, and grabbing Leo out of Tucker's crib, she lay back down in her bed and thought about her brother, willing herself to fall back to sleep as the horizon began to lighten with the coming of the sun.

She raised her arms to shield her eyes from the assaulting ice, once again standing on the frozen lake, the cold seeped thought her light slippers and pulled at her nightgown. She shivered against the wind and called out in frustration, repeating the steps by now she was pretty sure were useless.

"Vígolfr?" She tried to ignore the cold as it took her breath. "Why won't you help me? Why am I here?" She knew something was significant about this place, but she had no clue what it was. She'd never had a recurring dream so often and so vivid, but something about this place was sinister, and she did not want to be here. "What do I do?"

The wind answered her by picking up and throwing more snow and ice into her face. Isabella pulled her bathrobe closed, and looking around at the dark and empty horizon, she shrugged and turned her back to the wind.

"Best answer I'm going to get," she grumbled and began walking with the wind at her back. After walking for what seemed like hours, she saw snow-covered trees in the distance, and the wind started to lighten.

Isabella picked her way over the last few feet of the ice, and when her feet crunched into the snow on the bank of the lake, the wind died entirely, and she let her shoulders drop with a sigh of relief. It was still cold and creepy, but at least she was no longer being hit by flying pieces of ice and snow.

The scene wasn't much more encouraging—a thick dark forest bordering a rocky shore to the frozen lake. Layers of snow and ice covered everything on the bank except for some of the steeper borders. The edge of the forest was a mix of rocks, bushes, and smaller trees. She walked the shore and looked for a path she could take to find her brother, hopefully. Nothing. Not a single break in the impenetrable wall pulling at her bathrobe whenever she got close. In some of the thinner areas, Isabella could see deeper into the forest's gloom, but they didn't look much better. The shadows seemed to swell with menace, only held at bay by the brambles and the wind.

A rustling in the undergrowth caught her attention, and she backed away toward the lake until one of the boulders hit her in the back of the knees, and she sat down heavily on the cold stone. The rustling grew closer, and Isabella started to see some of the lower branches begin to move. Her breath caught in her throat as the creature neared the edge. When it burst from the pricker bush in front of her and tumbled head over tail, she couldn't help but laugh, more out of relief than amusement.

"Well then," the fox said, looking back at the offending pricker bush, "that's the last time I help you."

"Hello there," Isabella said, laughing at the little red fox standing on all fours in front of her.

The fox jumped at Isabella's voice and froze in place for only a moment before it began to run down the edge of the woods, bounding off the undergrowth, trying to find a way back in and away from her. When the fox was almost out of Isabella's sight, it stopped and turned around, sides heaving and puffs of breath coming from its open mouth.

Pushing off from the rock, Isabella followed the fox down the coast slowly. "It's okay little fox," she said, keeping her voice soft and non-threatening. "I just want to talk."

The fox watched her, eyes flittering around. As Isabella moved forward, the animal seemed to keep an eye out for an escape route, the underbrush appearing to be preferred. When she was within a few feet of the fox, it jumped again, spinning in the air, and began to run again, only to stop a little further down the coast, then turned and looked at Isabella, shoulders tense.

"It's okay," she said. "Want me to follow you?" Isabella took a few more steps toward the fox until her foot caught on a rock, and she stumbled forward, catching herself on her hands and knees, skinning the latter.

"Come on," she said, tears brimming in her eyes as she looked up to see the fox was gone. "I just wanted to– I just needed help. Please–" She sat down on the cold, snow-covered ground, ignoring the cold, wet seeping through her thin clothes. Placing her face in her hands, she let the anger and frustration flood out and drown all of her other senses. She stayed that way until she ran out of tears, and her shoulders stopped shaking from her sobs and started shaking because of the cold.

After a while, she felt a cold nose poking at her hands. Moving slowly, to avoid scaring the owner of the nose, Isabella moved her hands away from her face to find the little red fox sitting in front of her, watching.

"I take it you didn't want me to follow you," she said, her voice ragged from the cold and the crying.

The fox tensed and backed away a little at her voice, but when she didn't make any movement, it relaxed and inched forward again.

"What are you doing here?" the fox asked without so much as a hello. "You don't look strong enough to come here."

"I don't even know where here is."

"Not someplace a girl like you should be in a nightgown," the fox stood up whipping its tail toward her, then sat back down, smoothing its coat, and continued. "Aren't you cold?"

"Yeah, freezing."

"Then go home."

"I can't," Isabella said with a firmness in her voice she wasn't sure she felt, "I need to find my brother."

"Little two-legged guy?" The fox stood again and looked over its shoulder toward the woods, skipping sideways to a sound Isabella couldn't hear, before settling back on its haunches. "Wearing the sky?"

"Wearing the what?"

"The sky. Looked like the daytime sky."

"You mean, blue?" Isabella laughed.

"If that's what you call it."

"That's him," she felt hope swell in her heart for the first time since she'd awoken the morning Tucker had disappeared. "Where is he? Can you take me to him? Is he alright?"

"Slow down," the fox stood up and shuffled around in place as Isabella rapid-fired questions at it. "He is safe– for now. You need to find him quickly before they do."

"Before who finds him?"

"Not here," the fox shot a look at the trees again. "Find me later." The fox took off into the underbrush and was gone from sight.

Isabella sat up slowly in bed, squeezed her eyes shut, and threw Leo at Tucker's crib. The sun was up, and she knew she wouldn't be able to get back to sleep now. Any more searching would have to wait until tomorrow night. She didn't understand why the words of dream animals mattered so much, but she had a sneaking suspicion she needed to go back and find her brother. He was in there somewhere, and she could get him. She knew it.

EIGHT

"I can get it," Isabella said as her mother tried to pour the milk with trembling hands. "Why don't you go sit down."

"All I've been doing is sitting down," she said. "I need to do something."

Isabella didn't know what to say. She wanted to let her mother know about the dreams, but she remembered the look she'd given her father when Isabella had first mentioned the whole making a dream thing, and she could only imagine how her mother would judge her now. She knew this was something she would have to handle herself, at least until her father came home.

"When is Daddy going to be getting home?"

"I wish I knew," she said, looking at her cellphone, squinting and chewing her bottom lip, "I've been trying to get a hold of him all morning. His plane should have landed hours ago. You don't think–"

"No," Isabella didn't need to hear the rest of her mother's worries. She knew from the look on her face and the ringing of her hands she had gone to the darkest possible reasons. "No, Mom, he's fine. You know how his work is."

"True," her mother's distracted tone and crinkled forehead showed Isabella she didn't believe her.

Taking the carton of milk her mother had left on the counter, Isabella put it in the fridge before taking her plate to the table to eat her lunch. Across the table, her mother sat with her fifth cup of coffee, staring at her phone. That morning they had driven around and placed fliers all over town, then her mother had made several Facebook posts, hoping someone might see it and help Tucker get back to them. Isabella knew it wouldn't work because he wasn't out in the town somewhere. He hadn't been kidnapped and was too small to have run away. If any of it made sense, the only conclusion was he had become trapped in his dream, and if so, she needed to go in and get him.

Her mother's phone buzzed again, and she looked hopefully at the screen. She opened the notification, only to have her shoulders sag in the disappointment of simply another friend keeping them in their prayers or sharing the post again. It was hard to watch her mother keep getting her hopes up. Isabella didn't like not knowing where her father was either. He'd be able to help, be able to fix this, that was his thing. Isabella was getting just as worried as her mother. She didn't know where he was, and she didn't have any comforting words to play over in her head like she had for her brother: *He's safe for now.* Those words made it easier to deal with her brother still being missing, even if they had come with a vague warning about someone coming.

The ringing of her mother's phone made Isabella jump, knocking over her milk. "I'm sorry," she stammered, getting up to grab some paper towels to clean up her mess. "I didn't mean to– Whose on–" Her mother held up a hand to quiet her.

"Alright," her mother said into the phone, sitting up a little straighter in the chair. "Yes, we can do that.– No, thank you. I'm just glad you're safe." She took her phone from her ear and hung up, resting her forehead against the table.

"Mom," forgetting the paper towels mid-swipe, "everything okay?"

"That was your father," she said, the exhaustion heavy in her voice. "His delayed plane made him miss the connecting flight. It looks like he won't be home until tomorrow now," she looked up, tears glistening in her eyes, "now if we could find your brother."

"We will, Mom. I'm sure of it." Isabella walked over and hugged her mother.

"How," she sounded defeated and defenseless. In all her years, Isabella had never seen her mother so broken, "How do you know he'll be fine."

"I–" Isabella wanted to tell her mother, tell her everything. About her father weaving her dreams, about the dream she'd woven for Tucker. She ached to tell her the plan, how she would get him and bring him back. Tell her about the fox, about Vígolfr and his sister, about how they would help, tell her everything, and let her mother hold her and give her forgiveness. Instead, she stumbled for some lame reason, "I– I can't imagine anything else happening." Her tears began to flow unbidden, tears for her lies, tears for her mother, and tears for the loneliness she felt, knowing only she could bring her brother back.

Her mother turned to her and wrapped Isabella in her arms like she used to when she was younger and sat there at the kitchen table, each supporting the other's private grief and fear, neither knowing what the other was thinking, but none of it mattered at the moment. Isabella relaxed into her mother's embrace and rested her head on a shoulder she had cried on many times for reasons which now felt so small.

For the rest of the day, Isabella comforted her mother and took trips around the neighborhood with her, putting up fliers. By dinner, they were both exhausted, and while her mother was doing the dishes, Isabella let her mother know she was going to head up to bed, despite intending to get back to searching her dreams for her brother. While she had been comforted by the fox's claim, Tucker was alright, but the suggestion his safety was temporary nagged at her mind. During the afternoon, she had come up with the theory. If she gave herself the same dream she had given her brother, she should be able to find him.

Laying in her room, the covers pulled up tight under her neck, Isabella was having second thoughts. It seemed simple, give herself the same dream she gave her brother, then get him and bring him back. If Tucker went into the dream, there was no reason she couldn't do the same to herself, no reason except the chance of being trapped too. Shivering under the covers, she wondered if she should just wait for her father to come and help out. He must know how to fix this. The fox's warning echoed in her mind as she lay there in the darkness: *Find him quickly before they do.*

She rolled over and looked at Tucker's crib, blankets smoothed out, Leo tucked in like Tucker should have been. With a deep breath, Isabella rolled onto her back and closed her eyes. Breathing slowly, she pictured the field where she'd seen the horse in the dream her father had woven her, the one with the little stream, hoping it would be enough detail to get herself there. Isabella refrained from describing the gorgeous horse from the dream her father had given her, hoping to avoid another talking animal telling her what to do. She could feel sleep's tendrils pulling at her, and she let it drag her into the dream.

When she opened her eyes, Isabella was not in her bedroom, but she wasn't in the field either. Instead, she stood on the frozen lake, with no wind and no blue sky, alone in the darkness of the frozen lake, and the blank horizon stretched out all around her. She knew one of the directions would lead her to the edge of the woods where she'd met the fox, but she didn't know which direction.

"Vígolfr," she called out, listening to the silent night air for the answering howl.

All around her, the stars shone dimly in the clear night sky. The moon was barely a sliver and scarcely gave off enough light to see despite all the white snow and ice. The sound that came in answer to her call was evident in the crisp, still air, but the hollow response to her call was not the howl of a wolf. She could feel this sound deep in her chest, a cracking rumble causing the hairs on the back of her neck to stand up and goosebumps to flow across her skin.

An unformed darkness flowed across the ice until it floated just a few feet in front of her. Fear and despair ebbed from it in waves, and Isabella found herself taking an involuntary step backward. The shadow did not advance; instead, it floated where it was, intermittently blocking the stars dotting the night sky.

"Who– What are you?" Isabella struggled to form the words standing before this shadowy figure, and everything in her being told her to run. But she knew, like the wolf, she could not outrun this.

"You are being led astray, child," the shadow's voice sounded as empty as it looked. It paused as if waiting for a response, but Isabella didn't know what to say, so she stayed silent. "Do not trust Kimi. She will not tell you all she knows. Do not heed her warnings."

"I've never met Kimi," Isabella said, thinking of Vígolfr and his directive to find his sister who would help her get to her brother, but she didn't even know her name.

"Indeed," the voice sounded miles away, ebbing with the darker emotions flowing from the shadow. "She will find you, but I warn you, she will lead you from the path. She will make it harder to find your brother. You can only rely on yourself if you are going to save him."

"I don't even know where he is."

The shadow waved its ethereal arm over the ice, and a loud cracking sound echoed. The ice beneath Isabella's feet shuddered, sending her sprawling on all fours, her hand inches from a newly formed hole in the lake's surface. The icy water, splashing over the edges of the opening, numbed her hands, and she scrambled to her knees once the shuddering of the ice had stopped, tucking her hands in the armpits to warm them back to feeling.

Motion in the hole caught her attention, and the swirling water changed colors and stilled into the picture of a vibrant field covered with wildflowers with a gleaming train track running through it. In the middle of the area was a gentle stream. On one side of the stream was a small wooden cottage compete with a white picket fence and a clothesline like her grandmother used to have. On the other side of the stream was a dirt path leading into a dark forest with vibrant green trees lining the edges, but as her view zoomed out, the trees, deeper in the woods, changed to a sinister black, almost char like color, gnarled and barren.

The image zoomed back to the yard of the cottage, and there, sitting in the manicured grass, drinking what looked like apple juice, was her brother. He looked happy and safe within the fenced yard playing with a small wooden train, but he was clearly watching the gate, wondering what was beyond the relative safety of the yard. As she watched, he set down the juice box and began to walk toward the gate. The image started to fog over as the water refroze.

"No, wait," Isabella cried out as the image faded from view, replaced by the bare ice once more.

"His time is short," she shadow said. "Once he crosses from the greenery to the dark heart of the woods, he will be trapped in the dream world forever."

"Why are you telling me this? Why did you show me this and tell me where he is?"

"I have my reasons," the menace flowing from the shadow grew as it seemed to double in size before it dissolved into the night air, and Isabella woke up in her bed, drenched in sweat once more, the picture of the cottage burning white-hot in her head. Without delay, she pictured the cottage, the fenced-in yard, and the field of wildflowers with the train track running through it. Then her thoughts wandered to the stream and the path leading into the woods hiding their sinister secret, a secret told to her by the stuff of nightmares.

Now she was resolute. Now she knew where her brother was, and now she began to describe the scene aloud, weaving her fingers together in an intricate pattern that seemed more natural the more complicated it became. Sparks of blue light flashed briefly between her fingers as they got closer, and the room took on a light blue glow as she neared the end of her description. "It's now or never," she told herself before blowing into her now glowing hands and flattening them to her forehead.

NINE

The scene surrounding Isabella when she opened her eyes was both refreshing and terrifying. She lay on a soft lawn, grass tickling the back of her neck, and the earthy smell of a field just after a spring rain wafted through the air and made her smile. She closed her eyes again and breathed in the comforting warm air. Birds sang in the distance, and something frolicked in the grass nearby. She'd seen the place before, but her relief was once again dashed when she opened her eyes.

The sky was a deep blue with bright white clouds floating lazily in the breeze, but the tops of the trees she saw were an off-white tinged with yellows and blues. The grass had the same washed out, colorless appearance. The picture she had seen, the one she'd tried to imagine as she wove the dream together, was one of lush, vibrant greens. What she saw was almost a negative image of the scenes she had seen reflected in the frozen lake, and she worried this might be another dead end in the search for her brother.

A sound off to her right drew her attention, and she sat up, turning to get a better look at her surroundings. Everything around her stood out like an overexposed picture except the brightly painted picnic table, the intensely black tire swing hanging from the hauntingly pale tree, and the bright green door on the otherwise colorless cottage. She looked around the yard but could not see what had made the noise that drew her attention away from the strikingly blue sky, made more remarkable by the colorless world around her.

"Tucker," she called out, hoping he would respond with the infuriating Iee-iee he replaced her name with. "Tucker, buddy. Sister's here. You can come out."

She waited in the silence, the branches creaking in the light breeze, the only sound coming as her answer. A tinge of fear enveloped her as she remembered the warning the shadow had given her about the trees of the forest, the forest edge she could see paled in comparison to the lush green of the forest from her vision. Still, she couldn't let herself believe this was not the same place. She knew her brother was in trouble, if not at the moment, definitely soon, and she needed to get to him. If this wasn't the same place the shadow had shown her, she didn't know how to get there.

"Lost?" a familiar voice asked behind her.

Turning, Isabella looked down toward the brightly colored fox, made even brighter when in contrast to the white grass it sat in. "You're the fox from the pond, aren't you?"

"Yup," the fox said. "What are you doing here?"

"What do you mean?" Isabella looked around the clearing, searching desperately for a sign. "My brother, he's here somewhere."

"Are you so sure?" she fox got up and stretched lazily.

"Yes, I am," she snapped at the animal, "now help me to find him. You're the one who told me he's in danger."

"Actually, I think I told you he was safe."

"For now, but you said I needed to get to him before they did."

The fox looked back at the house and, bounding off toward the picnic table, called back to Isabella, "Little late now."

In the moments it took the fox's words to sink in, Isabella watched as the sleek creature jumped onto the top of the picnic table and stood there, looking out toward the gate of the cottage. Standing with her head held high, the fox looked majestic and powerful. Though clearly smaller than the wolf, the fox looked to have the same regal bearing of the arctic wolf. But as the words she had said sunk into Isabella, what initially looked majestic quickly shifted to smug. "Late?"

"Yup," the fox's nonchalance about the information annoyed Isabella, her brother's safety was at stake here, and this fox was just glibly telling her she was too late to help him.

"Where they did they take him?" Isabella looked around the clearing in more earnest, her sight falling upon the green door.

"Nowhere," the fox said as she curled up into a ball of red fur on the tabletop. "They left him right here. Well, it was over there more, in the grass, under the tree."

Isabella looked at the fox, her brow furrowed and her jaw slightly open. She felt a burning in her eyes, but refused to give into. "The grass," she felt all the color drain from her face, "is he—" the words were too difficult to utter, and she let the sentence drop into the silence between them. Each step, toward the place the fox had indicated with her nose before curling up, felt to Isabella like walking upstream through a river. She didn't know what she was expecting to find, but the ominous words of the fox made her realize she probably didn't want to see.

The lone tree in the yard stood even with the cottage roof, blue-white fruit, about the size and shape of an apple, hung from the branches. A black tire hung on yellow ropes from one of the lower limbs, swinging gently in the breeze. Isabelle noticed the slight change in the light as it struggled to find a way through the white leaves hanging from the branches. With more effort than it should have taken, she stood next to the tire and looked on the ground around the tree. Over by the trunk, a bit away from where she stood, something lay in the grass.

Relief flooded through her as she realized the green box discarded in the pale grass was a juice box, the tell-tale straw still dangling from the top. She picked up the small box, and a series of images flashed through her mind.

Tucker swinging on the tire. The green door opening. Three kids running over to him. Faces blurred. Words she couldn't make out. Excited voices melding together. Hands helping him down. Spinning. Running. Laughing. The spinning world. Vibrant greens and browns and blues. The blue sky. They hand him something– the juice box. Sitting in the grass. Voices were calling to him from the gate.

She came back to the tree. Its bark had a silver hue to it, glistening in the sun. She reached out to touch it but hesitated and dropped the green box back into the pale grass. Her attention returned to the fox still curled, unconcerned, on the table across the yard.

"Who were they?"

The fox stretched and yawned, "Who?"

Isabella stared at the door to the cottage, "Is he in there?"

"The cottage?"

"No, the tree," Isabella snapped, "of course."

"Well, he's not in the tree."

Isabella sighed and glared at the fox, turning her back on the table. With her shoulders squared in defiance, she marched toward the door. If her brother was in there, getting him out was her top priority, no matter who those kids are. If he is in danger, it was her fault, and she will get him out of it. The closer she got to the door, the less sure she felt, but she did not let her doubt stop her. Stepping up onto the front steps, Isabella reached out to grab the doorknob feeling a static charge as her hand closed on the metal knob.

"I wouldn't do that," the fox said lazily from the table across the yard.

"Oh, you wouldn't, would you?" She turned, trying not to show her relief at moving away from the door, and stalked across the yard until she stood at the edge of the picnic table. "What exactly would you do then? All you have done so far is lay on this stupid table and criticize me. Who do you think you are anyway?"

The fox stood up, as if it had been waiting for this invitation the whole time, and lowering its head until its chin touched the table, she said, "They call me Kimi. It is a pleasure to finally meet you properly."

"Kimi," Isabella's memory shot back to what the shadow had said, "I've heard of you."

"Have you now," Kimi stood up and cocked her head to the right with a look of confusion on her face, "I'd only believe half of it if I were you."

"Oh, you'd like that, wouldn't you," Isabella stomped her foot. With one last glare at Kimi standing on the tabletop, she turned and headed straight back to the door. New confidence she was making the right choice firmly in her heart helped her push aside the uneasy feeling she had as she grasped the doorknob, the static shocking her palm, and threw open the door.

On the other side of the door was the mirror image of the yard she stood in, only instead of the washed-out versions of the livid world she'd seen in the ice, and when she picked up the juice box, the vibrant colors seemed almost too bright after having been in the muted world around her. Her breath caught in her throat as the luxurious colors flowed out before her. Leaving the door open, Isabella took a step back and walked around the side of the house, half expecting to see the vibrant colors hidden by a thin wall, but instead, she saw the dull side of the blueish-white cottage walls. She looked through the window and saw a kitchen, complete with table and appliances, similarly muted in color to everything else on this side of the door. When she got back to the door, the fox was standing on the stoop, watching her.

"You wouldn't do that, eh?" Isabella asked, "You're not going to stop me from getting my brother."

"Wouldn't dream of it," Kimi said, looking through the door at something under the green tree with bright shining red apples dangling from its branches.

Isabella followed her gaze and saw, sitting under the tree stacking the fallen apples on top of each other, her brother sat in his footed pajamas. The shock of crazy blond hair catching the sun as it filtered through the lively leaves covering the branches of the too big apple tree.

"Tucker," Isabella whispered, and tears of joy pooling in her eyes. She rushed forward through the door, almost tripping over Kimi as they stepped through the doorway together. "Tucker," she called louder, ignoring the sound of the door slamming behind her. He looked up from his stacked apples and waved with a huge smile on his face.

"Apples," he shouted in his exuberance, "Iee-iee, apples!" He stood up, Leo grasped tightly under his arm.

"Tucker, I'm so glad you're safe," Isabella ran down the stairs and toward her brother, but as she got to him and tried to sweep him up into her arms for a hug, he evaporated into a shimmering mist. "Tucker," she called out, searching for him in the yard.

"I don't like this," Kimi said at Isabella's heels.

"Nobody asked you," Isabella said to Kimi. Spotting her brother over at the gate of the yard, she called, "Tucker, wait, buddy. We have to go home."

"Hide and seek," he called back to her.

"You don't want to go out there," Kimi warned, "this isn't right."

"Again," Isabella turned to look at the fox, "didn't ask. Why don't you just go lay down and leave me alone? I've been warned about you."

"You keep saying," Kimi looked up at Isabella, "but I don't feel comfortable here, so I'm gonna stick by you if it's all the same."

"It's not," she turned back toward the now empty gate. "Great, now you made me lose him. You're a bundle of help."

"Maybe if you listened once in a while, I would be."

"Or maybe you're trying to keep me from getting my brother," she snapped at the fox. "Besides, you're part of my dream, you're not even real, and animals don't talk, so just leave me alone and let me get my brother."

Kimi flinched at Isabella's words and, with an audible huff, turned and walked away into the longer grass around the fence. Isabella watched her go with a pang of regret. As annoying and unhelpful as she had been, it was nice not to be alone in this strange place. She turned her attention back to the gate, where she had last seen her brother, and smiled, remembering the last thing she'd heard him say.

"I'm it, I guess." Isabella jogged toward the gate, out of the yard, and away from the little yellow cottage in the clearing.

⤞ TEN ⤝

The gate squealed behind her, complaining on its hinges in a way it hadn't when Tucker went through. Isabella let it slam back into the fence and headed straight out into the long grass surrounding the cottage. She couldn't see Tucker as he ran through the grass, but she could see the long grass moving in the distance. His giggling cut through the quiet air, teasing her on as it grew louder or faded depending on how close she got to the waving grass.

"Tucker," she called out, trying hard to keep her voice playful despite the rising panic she felt, "I don't want to play hide and seek."

"Hide and seek," his voice echoed hers.

"Tucker, buddy," she said as she neared the space where the grass was moving, "I gotcha!" She said, jumping to the area just in time to see the grass close on his blond head as he tunneled through to another place, sending a path of shivering grass after him. "Come on," Isabella said, looking at the cloudless blue sky.

A rustling in the grass over to her left caught her eye this time. She crashed through the field, tripping twice over unseen roots until she jumped into the area where the grass had been moving, her foot grabbing on the metal rail of a train track, causing her to tumble forward. Catching herself before she hit the opposite rail with her head, she clambered up, arms out, ready to catch her brother before he scurried away, but once again, all she saw was his blond hair bobbing through the grass ahead of her. "Tucker," she called out after him, giggling was his only answer. This cat and mouse game went on three more times before Isabella jumped into a lower spot in the grass, and sitting in the middle was the red fox, its colors muted against the bright green of the field.

"It's you," Isabella said with more anger than she meant to. The game of hide-and-seek was getting annoying, and now to have Kimi trick her off of her brother's trail was adding insult to injury. "I almost got him. Why are you distracting me?"

Before Kimi could answer, her brother's giggle a few feet away caught her attention, and she dove for the area, her hands falling once again on the cold steel of the train track. "Tucker," the frustration was evident in her voice this time. She was running in circles trying to get him, but every time she got close, she'd see him speed off through the grass again.

As she was standing up, Kimi walked through the grass, slow and silent, and when she spoke, Isabella jumped, "You won't get him."

"Is that a threat?" Isabella stood, putting her hands on her hips and looking down at the sleek red fox.

"It is what you see it as."

"Well, I will tell you something," Isabella fought back the tears of frustration, "you can't stop me from doing this. I need to save my brother."

"Well, it's obvious," the fox's voice seemed to be equal parts annoyance and condescension, which infuriated Isabella, who turned and stalked away into the taller grass looking for movement.

When she saw the swaying grass shiver, she took off at a run, ignoring as the tall stalks of grass seed whipped against her. She plowed through the field toward the edge of the woods. Once again, she jumped at the empty air. She stood there, breathing heavily, hands on her knees. Isabella knew chasing her brother through the grass wasn't working, but Tucker wasn't listening, so she didn't have much choice except to play his game.

After catching her breath, she scanned the top of the grass again, looking for the movement. The soft, uniform swaying of the grass was more than she could take, and everything came crashing down on her. The frustration with the fox, the annoyance with her brother's childishness, the anger at her father for not being here when she needed him, but most of all, the fear she would never see any of them again. She let all of her pent-up emotion out as she called at the top of her lungs, "Tucker Shaw, you get your butt back here right this minute. I am not playing."

A giggle in the distance answered her outburst, which only infuriated her more. "I'm serious! This isn't funny." A clear path of shivering grass showed up again, back closer to the cottage, and Isabella took off toward it.

"Tucker, wait," she panted against her burning chest. Each step back toward the cabin was like walking through deepening sand, and the faster Isabella tried to move, the slower she was able to. When she finally got to the last place the grass had been moving, she saw Kimi smugly sitting there, just outside the gate, waiting for her. "You," the tears of frustration burned down her cheeks. "Stop trying to lead me away from my brother."

"Why do you keep coming to where I am?" the fox asked in return.

"What? You keep— I'm just, following— Ugh" her fists shot down to her sides as she stammered in frustration, stamping her foot with the last word. She spun on her heels and called out to her bother. The silence was complete following her call. Not even the grass swaying in the winds made a sound as she waited for his words or his laugh to pierce the air.

"Tucker," she called. "Tucker." The strain in her voice was becoming impossible to hide. Each time she called his name, tears of frustration and anger pushed further to the surface, until she was finally standing there, hoarsely croaking his name, positive she had lost him once again, terrified she would never be able to find him.

"If you're done with this," Kimi said, still sitting at her feet, "we should get going."

"If I'm done," she turned on the fox with such anger. She thought about kicking the small creature away from her, but despite her hatred for the condescending creature, she couldn't bring herself to hurt it. "Just leave me alone," she said and walked through the gate, slamming it behind her.

Isabella walked over to the tree, sat down against its deep brown trunk, and buried her face in her hands. The sweet smell of overripe apples clung to the area like a blanket. She sat for a time listening to her own hitched breaths as exhaustion overwhelmed her. For the first time, she noticed the complete lack of sound, no birds singing, no creaking of the gate, no swaying grass in the wind, just her breath and the soft whimpers escaping her every so often when the tears became too much.

When she had finally gotten ahold of her tears, she wiped her face with the sleeve of her pajamas and leaned her head back against the tree, letting her arms fall to the dirt at her side. She closed her eyes and sat there, hoping when she opened them she would once again be in her bedroom back into a reality not much better than this nightmare, but at least there she wasn't alone. She slowed her breathing and imagined herself in her bedroom, laying under her covers tucked safely in the room she'd recently shared with her brother. While she tried to imagine the soft pillow beneath her head, a cold, wet nose prodded her hand from the dirt, and the warm course fir of the fox replaced the cold hard ground under her hand. Absently, Isabella stroked the fir, her anxiety and loneliness easing as she did.

"As much as I am enjoying this," Kimi said after a few moments, "I think we should get going."

Isabella's shoulders went rigid, and her jaw tightened. She pushed the fox away with her hand and practically growled, "I am not leaving without Tucker."

The fox walked a few feet away and sighed. Immediately, Isabelle's tensions and fears hammered down on her, and once again, she glared at the fox with such menace, she picked up an apple and threw it at the little animal. This time she meant to hit it. She would have used something more substantial, too, if there was anything around. Kimi easily evaded the apple and stood a little further off, silently watching Isabella as she pulled her knees up to her chest and rested her head on them in utter defeat.

Isabella wasn't angry with the fox; in fact, she agreed with it, but that was the problem. She was ready to leave, abandon her brother to whatever this place was, and she hated herself for it. Her parents would never forgive her for abandoning her little brother in some strange field, knowing it was all her fault. She couldn't cry, there just weren't the tears for it anymore, but she couldn't forgive herself either. She was giving up, and she wanted to blame the fox, Kimi, for it, but blaming her wasn't entirely fair either. She had tried to get to her brother, but she wasn't fast enough, it was just too hard for her, and once again, she had failed.

These thoughts were spinning through her head when the first scream pierced the silent air. It was a scared, hollow sound, the sound of something caught in a trap, knowing the hunter was on its way. The sound of hopeless fury that only comes at the end when you have given up on everything and the only thing left is the tears. Her head snapped up at the sound, not because it sounded like her brother's voice, but because it didn't. This was the first sound in this place that wasn't her brother, her, or Kimi, and it made the hairs on her arm stand up. She glanced at Kimi, standing in on the stone path leading from the cottage to the gate. Her lips were pulled back in a snarl, revealing small but sharp fangs, reminding Isabella although she could talk, Kimi was an animal, and animals had instincts people didn't. Something dangerous was coming. She looked between Kimi and the gate.

"What is it, Kimi?"

"I don't know," the fox said, interrupting the low growl she had been emitting. "I also don't want to find out."

"But my brother's out there."

"If he's out there with that, there's not much we can do to help him."

"But—"

"But I don't think he was ever out there, to begin with."

"What do you mean?" Isabella looked at the Kimi closely for the first time. Her face was gentle, despite the teeth currently bared toward the field. Teeth she had never once barred to Isabella, despite the words, and the apple, she'd thrown at the animal. Her eyes were gentle and intelligent, and every time they glanced at Isabella, affection glistened in those dark irises.

"I mean what I said," she sifted her gaze back to the gate, and all affection twisted into fierce hatred that made Isabella flinch. "Can we go now?"

Another scream pierced the still air, just as sad and painful as before. Isabella wanted to convince herself it came from some animal, some trapped or wounded thing living in the woods or the field, but there was a human quality to the voice Isabella couldn't ignore. She was comforted because the scream didn't sound like her brother, but she didn't buy Kimi's suggestion that Tucker was never here. She'd seen him with her own eyes. He was out there somewhere, with whatever was screaming out there. Kimi was right about one thing though, she couldn't do anything about it for now. The sound of the screams chilled her to the bone and weighed on her heart in a way she couldn't quite name. She didn't want to know what would happen if she saw the thing making that sound.

"Yeah," Isabella stood up, not taking her eyes off the gate. A low rumbling sound started on the horizon, so low she could feel it in her chest. "Yeah, I think it's time to go."

ELEVEN

T he rumbling grew more intense, and Isabella had to put her hand on the tree to steady herself on the shaking ground. Eyes glued on the distant trees, she was frozen in place, watching as a cloud of dirt and dust billowed all along the horizon. "Tucker," she whispered, her voice stolen by the weight of the emotions baring down on her.

"The door would probably be a good idea right about now," Kimi said, backing along the path toward the cottage. "A really, really good idea."

The shaking ground knocked some of the apples off of the tree, causing them to bounce and roll at Isabella's feet. It wasn't until the rumbling became a tremendous tearing roar so loud it sounded like the sky was being ripped from the earth— and given the growing dust cloud, Isabella couldn't be sure it wasn't—that her trance was broken. She moved toward the cottage and the red door with careful steps around the shaking, apple strewn ground. Her last several steps were more of a stumble up the stairs as another tearing shook the land.

Isabella grabbed the knob as much to keep from falling to the ground as to open the door. She looked at her feet, where the fox paced impatiently. Thoughts of Tucker ran through her head, his laughter, his nightly cries, and her heart broke with the idea of not seeing him again. She sucked in a deep breath and turned the knob. The doorknob jerked a little to the right but stopped and held fast.

"Any minute now," Kimi said, her voice almost lost in the near-constant tearing sound coming from all around them.

"It's locked," Isabella jiggled the knob some more, but nothing happened. She banged on the door, threw her shoulder at it, but the door didn't even shudder.

The little fox gave a menacing growl as she paced around Isabella's legs. "I knew this was a bad idea."

"I had to get my brother," Isabella pleaded. "He was in here, and I needed to get him."

"How's that working for you?" The fox asked before it bounded around the house, oblivious to Isabella's furious stare, returning moments later. "The same on all sides."

"What do we do?"

"Not come in here in the first place?" The fox sat by the corner of the house, looking toward the gate. "Seeing as we are here, I guess you need to think of something."

"Me?"

"In case you haven't noticed, I don't have any thumbs. Tools are your department," the fox said, motioning over to the shuddering apple tree.

Along with the apples, some of the branches had started to snap and fall to the ground. Isabella rushed to grab the largest one she could lift, a short stick about as thick as the fox's tail. She held it like a softball bat and took a swing at the door. The branch reverberated off the wood, causing her to drop the stick. A soft voice called Isabella's name behind her, and she turned around to look at the gate and the field beyond. It sounded like Tucker, but she wasn't sure over all the other noise enveloping the area.

"Tucker," she asked as she abandoned the door and walked toward the gate, oblivious of the shaking ground. "Tucker, you out there?"

"Iee-iee," a soft voice called, "where are you?"

"Tucker," Isabella reached the gate, her hand on the metal as she pushed it open, thinking only of finding her brother.

"Don't go out there," Kimi called, running after her. "You'll never make it in time."

"But Tucker's out there."

"Then call him, and tell him to come to you. That's the only way any of us will make it out of here."

Isabella looked at the approaching dust cloud, the thunderous roar growing every moment. Then her eyes drifted back toward the cottage and the locked door. She knew Kimi was right. If she didn't get the door open, it wouldn't matter if she found her brother. None of them would get out of here. "Tucker," she called over the roar, "Tucker buddy, you need to come to my voice. Come back to the cottage." She backed away from the gate. The shaking in the ground redoubled, and by the time she was halfway back to the door, Isabella was almost crawling. She picked up the branch and slammed it into the door, screaming Tucker's name with each successive hit, each time the stick shuttered, but the door didn't budge. Eventually, she dropped the branch on the doorstep and started banging on the door with her fists.

Kimi walked next to her, the tension noticeable in the fox's movements. "Think maybe there's another way?"

"How should I know?" Isabella looked around the fenced yard, leaning against the house for support as the ground shuddered violently again. A rattling caught her attention, and without another word, she picked up the stick and threw it through the kitchen window.

"Another way," Kimi nodded.

Isabella hoisted herself through the window, expecting to be transported back into the whitewashed world, but instead, she landed heavily on a dirty wooden floor next to a kitchen table. She scrambled to her feet, dusting herself off, and unlocked the kitchen door from the inside. Kimi was sitting on the doorstep, looking up at Isabella with what could pass as a smile. "Now what?"

"How do I know?" The insult in the fox's voice was hard to miss, "I didn't make this place."

"Are you suggesting I did?"

"I sure hope not," Kimi walked past her into the kitchen. "If you did, we are going to need to have a nice long talk when we get out of here."

"What happens if we don't get out of here?" Isabella's answer came from another long ripping sound. She watched as the last of the field outside the fence fell away into the black void now surrounding the yard. "Tucker," the word tore from her throat.

"Iee-iee," his voice sounded far away, "I want apple."

"Tucker," hope flared in her chest as she searched for her brother around the shaking branches of the tree.

"Help me," he called.

"I've found it," Kimi said from the back of the kitchen, "come get this door open. We need to get out of here before there's no more here to get out of."

Isabella looked back and forth between her brother and the fox standing in front of a blue door. She needed to see if that door was locked too. If it was, there could be something in the kitchen to open it, but time was falling away quickly like the ground outside. "Tucker," she called out of the open front door, "come on in the cabin. We're going to get out of here." She turned her back to the door and headed deeper into the kitchen.

In the kitchen hall, Isabella found a door like the one she used to enter the cottage, except blue. Kimi paced in front of the door, looking like a pet needing to go out to pee. Isabella reached for the knob, the same static shock from before buzzed through her, and she knew this was the right door. The knob turned with ease, and as she pulled the door open, a relieved Kimi rushed through the opening into the whitewashed world beyond. Isabella stood in the doorway, her hand on the handle, and turned to look at the open front door.

"Iee-iee," Tucker's voice called from beyond the open front door, "look at me."

Isabella looked back and forth between the two open doors.

"Come through," Kimi called to her, "what are you waiting for?"

"I can't," Isabella turned to the front door, "I need to get Tucker first."

"There's no time for this," the fox's pinned her ears back and glared at Isabella.

"I'm not leaving here without him," Isabella called over her shoulder and sprinted for the front door. When she reached the opening, she had to shield her face from the flying dust and debris. A cracking rumble shook the cottage causing plaster and dust to rain through the kitchen, and the fence surrounding the lawn fell away into the ever-expanding cavern forming around her. Cracks spidered through the yard, running under the picnic table and through the roots of the oversized apple tree. "Tucker," she called out, steadying herself on the red door frame.

"Up here," a small voice came from the canopy of the tree. "Look at me."

Isabella scanned the tree branches trying to find her brother, and without thinking, she stepped out of the house and began down the path toward the ever-nearing cliff. A tug on her nightgown drew her eyes away from the tree. Kimi was there, teeth sunk into the fabric of her pajamas, trying to pull Isabella back toward the cottage with all her might.

"Leave me alone," Isabella tried to push Kimi away with her foot, being careful not to hurt her, "I need to get Tucker. He loves to climb. He's in the tree."

"We need to go," she said, letting go of the fabric for just long enough to talk, then latching her teeth back in, refusing to let go.

"Tucker, come down," Isabella reached the trunk of the tree. The tire swing lay on the ground, its branch having broken away when a fissure shook the tree's roots. "I can't climb up to get you."

"We need to go now," Kimi said through clenched teeth, relentlessly pulling at the hem of the nightgown.

The ground shuddered violently, and the trunk of the tree splintered, sending half of the tree over the edge. Isabella screamed and reached out for the rest of the tree, grabbing a lower branch as it began to topple over. With a rending crack, the branch she held snapped from the tree as it toppled over the edge of the cliff. Bright sun shone through the empty branches. Isabella dropped to her knees, staring into the abyss in front of her. Kimi pulled on her nightgown, whimpering and urging her back, but Isabella had gone numb. She had failed everyone, her brother, her parents, this was all her fault, and now she couldn't do anything to fix it. The whole world went silent as she knelt on the edge of the abyss, the ground crumbling beneath her.

Sharp pain in her hand snapped the world back into noisy focus. She looked down at the small dots of blood pooling on the back of her hand. Next to her was an apologetic-looking Kimi, whimpering and shaking.

"We need to go," she looked over her shoulder at the darkness surrounding them, "and I'm not going without you."

Isabella looked at the soft red fox, large gentle eyes stared back at her expectantly. The ground began to crumble, and with one last look out over the cliff, Isabella grabbed Kimi in her arms and, standing on unsteady feet, ran for the cottage and the open blue door inside. The ground crumbled at her heels, sending splintering cracks through the kitchen floorboards. Burst pipes sent water streaming through the air, dirt trapped between the second story's floorboards filtered through the air, and splintering boards cracked. The cottage's front wall tore away from the building with angry snapping sounds sending large chunks of plaster and wooden beams crashing to the floor around them. With one last leap, pushing off as the floor fell away beneath her feet, Isabella propelled herself through the falling blue door, landing hard on the blue-tinted grass, hitting the firm and steadfast ground. Kimi flew from her arms and rolled away, landing in a violent tumble.

Sitting up, Isabella turned around in time to see the off-white cottage collapse in on itself, splinters and dust roiling up in a plume toward the bright blue sky, momentarily hiding the cotton ball clouds from view. At first billowing in the air, the dust was sucked down toward the wreckage, which pulled in on itself until there was nothing left but a square of dirt.

TWELVE

W hat was that?" Isabella stared at the square of dirt where the house had once stood. There was nothing there. No broken wood, no pools of water, not even so much as a fragment remained from the little cottage from which she had just dove.

"That was a dream trap," Kimi said as she limped up to Isabella's side.

"A trap," Isabella's hand flew to her mouth, "Tucker was in there. What happened to him?"

"Hard to say," Kimi sat down in the grass, "depends on the trap."

"Is he— is he dead?" The tears were fighting at the back of Isabella's eyes, threatening to open up the floodgates.

"Doubt it," Kimi's ears perked up, and she turned her head toward the gate behind them.

Isabella looked at her expectantly. "You doubt it? Are you planning on explaining why you doubt he's dead given the place we were in just fell apart and the house just imploded?"

Kimi turned her attention to Isabella, "Nope, wasn't planning on it." Then she stood up quickly and took off across the faded, blue-tinted grass toward the gate.

"Hey," Isabella called after her. When she didn't answer, Isabella rolled her eyes and stood up, stretching the soreness out of her left leg, and jogged after the sleek creature. "Hey there, wait up."

Kimi stopped at the gate to the world beyond and looked back over her shoulder. "You'll just slow me down," she said and then squeezed through the fence and zipped through the field until Isabella couldn't see the grass moving anymore.

By the time Isabella got to the gate, she stood looking over a field of blue-white grass, standing about three feet tall and swaying gently in the breeze. Birds sung in the distant trees, and the grass swished as it swayed in the wind. She realized these sounds hadn't existed on the other side of the blue door. "A dream trap," she repeated to herself. "Whatever that is."

She pushed open the gate, which glided smoothly on well-oiled hinges, very different than on the other side, and was about to set foot beyond the confines of the cottage. A flash of the ground falling away ran through her mind. Stepping through the gate had started the destruction last time, and there was no place to go if it happened again. She hesitated, her foot hanging in the air over the threshold of the fence. Putting her foot back down on her side of the fence, she let the gate close and stood there studying the scene around her. The sky was blue, and the clouds looked ordinary, but all of the grass and trees were a strange whitish color edged with blue.

Nothing about this place made any sense to her. Kimi, the fox, seemed to have wanted to help her, but the shadow from the other dream had told Isabella not to trust her. Isabella didn't know which to believe. Kimi had gotten her out of the dream trap, but she had also stopped Isabella from rescuing her brother. Now he was trapped in some alternate sunken dream, or worse. She shook her head to get the thought away. She knew there was something Kimi wasn't telling her, she'd doubted Tucker was dead, which was good, but there are worse things than death. It was Kimi's fault Tucker was stuck in the trap, and it was up to Isabella to find a way to get him out and back to their parents.

She took a deep breath and pushed through the gate, ready for whatever trap she was going to spring. She needed to rescue Tucker, and she wasn't going to accomplish anything hiding behind the fence. Stepped through the gate, Isabella covered her eyes from the sun's glare. When the worst had passed, she took down her hand and looked around at the vibrant greens and browns surrounding her. The world had popped back into color.

She looked down at herself and noticed she was no longer dressed in her nightgown and bare feet. Somehow she was now wearing a loose white blouse under her black hooded faux leather jacket, jeans, and her cowboy boots, bright yellow flowers embroidered down the side. While surprised, she was a little relieved; the thought of running around the field searching for her brother in the nightgown hadn't been the most appealing thing about this, not that there was much good going on, to be honest.

A breeze from behind made her turn in time to see the whole yard twinkle and fade from view. Left in its place was an unblemished field of vibrant green grass, about three feet tall. She searched the area for any sign of the apple tree or the yard, but all she could see around her was a lush, vibrant field of green grass bisected by shining train tracks. The sky above remained a bright blue, housing several puffy sheep's wool clouds. Birds sang in the distance, and far at the edge of the field, a thin line of smoke rose. Isabella watched the smoke, half expecting it would spread to envelop the entire horizon, trapping her in the middle of its path, but that didn't happen. Instead, the smoke rose peacefully into the calm sky.

She wondered if she should head there and find other people who could help her find her brother. It looked far away, but Tucker wasn't going anywhere. She needed to get the house back; if Kimi was right, and Tucker was still alive somewhere, there could be someone where the smoke was who could help her. Of course, the smoke could also be from whoever set the dream trap, as Kimi had called it. Isabella was torn, so instead of heading for the smoke, she sat in the grass and pulled it up from the roots.

Tucker needed someone to rescue him, but she wasn't a hero. Heroes were people who valiantly came to the rescue of people like her. At best, she was a victim, possibly the villain, and Tucker wouldn't be in this situation if she hadn't trapped him in this world if that is even what happened. She couldn't make sense of anything, and the only person she'd been able to talk to this whole time was a rather vague fox.

Squeezing her eyes shut, Isabella willed herself to wake up. Somewhere in the real world, she was sleeping in her bed, but the birds continued to sing, and the breeze pushed gently on her back. Isabella wondered what would happen if she just simply sat there and waited for someone to come help. Someone would come, she tried to convince herself of the fact, listing the ways they could find her. Maybe she was in a coma in the real world, and her mother would take her to the doctors, they'd wake her up, and she could go back to living her life.

It was all a pleasant thought if she didn't think too deeply about it. She'd be home, but her brother would still be missing, her mother depressed, and her father would probably be disappointed if he found out what she did. She wasn't sure he would ever be able to forgive her. Putting her head in her hands, Isabella pushed up from the ground and stood, resolution filling her stance. She pushed back the hair the wind was blowing in her face, licked her lips, and started forward, toward the edge of the forest. No one was coming to help her, there was no real doubt about that, so there was no reason to find out whose smoke was in the distance. Instead, forward toward the stream, she had seen when the shadow had shown where her brother was.

She had listened to Kimi back in the trap, but they had failed to rescue Tucker. Isabella wouldn't make the same mistake again. The shadow had been right all along. Kimi was not a friend, she reminded herself. The little fox was more concerned about saving herself than about helping Isabella. That wasn't the kind of help she wanted or needed. If she was going to rescue her brother, she knew she'd have to do it alone.

With fresh determination, she set out toward the edge of the woods, knowing a short time before she would arrive at the forest, there would be the water. It had looked shallow, and she breathed a sigh of relief because she'd always had a strange fear of water, so she's actively avoided learning to swim. The thought of swimming across hadn't been high on her list of activities, even in a dream.

After a short trip through the grass, Isabella found what she'd remembered as a wandering stream, but now, closer up, it looked more like a rambling river, bisecting the field. The water moved swiftly through what looked like a deep gouge in the field, but it wound gracefully along through the field, reflecting the cerulean sky. Isabella looked across the river and chewed on her lip, a habit her parents hated but helped her focus. The river was broader and deeper than she'd assumed from what the shadows had shown her, and unless she could find a bridge, a boat, or a shallow section to cross, she knew she'd never make it.

Movement on the other side of the river caught her attention, and her breath caught in her throat when she saw Tucker pick up a small stone and try to skip it across the water. His stone barely went a foot into the water with an unsatisfying plunk.

"Tucker," Isabella called from across the river. "Tucker, I'm here to take you home."

He didn't answer her. Instead, he picked up another small stone and examined it. He was focused on the pebble while Isabella called him, desperate to hear his voice. Seeming satisfied with the stone, Tucker drew his arm back over his head and threw the stone into the shallows of the river.

"Tucker," she tried again, "stay put. I'm coming to get you." How he was even here, Isabella couldn't figure out, but she was happy he was. Now, if he could just hear her. She searched the bank and the water frantically, yet unsuccessfully, to find a way she could cross here, where she could keep an eye on Tucker. "Stay here, buddy," she called, knowing she had to find another place to cross, "I'll be right back."

That said, albeit unheard, Isabella turned down the edge of the river and ran, searching for someplace she would be able to get across. Her feet carried her along the bank, kicking sand and mud up as she wound her way with the river toward the thin line of smoke rising in the distance. Heading toward the smoke was risky because the smoke could be the person who had set the trap she'd almost fallen prey to, but as far as she could see, there weren't many other options. There was no way she would be able to cross the water as it was.

Glancing back at Tucker, she saw he'd gotten bored with throwing the stones, and he'd started to explore other parts of the river bank. She was afraid he might fall in, but most importantly, she was scared he would head into the forest. The shadow had warned her about the trees deeper in the woods. If Tucker wandered into that section, he would never be able to come out. She knew it was true. She was sure of it. The shadow had not led her astray yet. She'd found the juice box he was drinking when she first saw him through the hole in the ice. It had been in a trap, but the shadow couldn't have known.

"Tucker," she knew he wouldn't hear her, but she had to try, "Tucker, stay out of the woods, buddy. Don't go in there. Stay by the river, and I'll come get you." Tucker looked up as if he heard something, then stood and started toward the edge of the woods. Isabella's heart skipped when she spotted the path about halfway between them. Tucker was headed toward the woods in the opposite direction, but he'd find it eventually. He was a curious kid, and she knew he'd find it, probably sooner than later.

She turned toward the smoke and dug her heels in, running as fast as she could toward the most likely place to cross. Whoever was there may have a boat, or it could be a shallow area. Tucker had to have gotten over there somehow, and if he could do it, so could she. "I'm coming, buddy," Isabella told the river as she ran, "just stay safe until then."

❧ THIRTEEN ❧

As she got closer, the smoke she'd thought was one stream turned into several smaller ones from the chimneys of small cottages. A little further in, Isabella found herself at a fountain. In the middle of what seemed to be a bustling market. People moved through the streets with carts covered with strange-looking fruit and vegetables while others were opening large windows from their shops onto the wide dirt road running along the river. She had to move out of more than a couple of people's way as they hurried through their morning routine.

The buildings on either side of the street, though more were on the side away from the water, were low and made of bare wood, like something you would see in an old western town, without the saloon and shootouts. Except for the apparent lack of modern conveniences, the village seemed entirely unremarkable. The most advanced piece of technology Isabella could see was a waterwheel churning in the river.

"Can you help me?" Isabella tapped one woman pushing a cart full of bread through the street. The woman kept moving, pushing her cart over to the side of the road and locking the wheel before setting up her shop for the day. Isabella watched, expecting the woman to answer any minute. "Excuse me?"

The woman didn't answer; instead, she started calling out about bread for sale. On his way to the bread cart, one man tried walking through Isabella, forcing her to move aside. Still, the woman didn't respond to Isabella. Offended, she stalked up to the woman's cart and turned the woman to look at her. The woman's eyes were glazed over, and she seemed to look through Isabella as if she weren't there. Letting the woman's shoulder go, she watched as the bread seller turned back to her cart and continued her conversation with the customer as if nothing had just happened.

As Isabella moved through the crowded street, each interaction basically the same. Most people just ignored her, while some reacted with mild annoyance. No one was outright hostile toward her, but several people shot dirty looks her way as they grumbled on their way past. Desperate for answers and more than a little frustrated, Isabella sat down on the village center's fountain, just across a roughly paved stone plaza from the waterwheel. She tried to talk to everyone who came to gather water from the well, hoping that someone would eventually respond to her.

"Are you alright, child?" An old woman, dressed in brightly colored clothes and jingling bracelets almost up to her elbows, asked Isabella as she sat on the edge of the fountain. "You look a little lonely."

"You noticed?" Isabella asked, surprising herself with how relieved she felt to be acknowledged with kindness.

"Of course, my girl," she sat down on the edge of the fountain, "how could I not notice you? Even with your current sad and lonely state, I can't help but notice there is greatness right here," she poked her finger into Isabella's chest.

"I wasn't sure anyone here saw me." Isabella looked at the cart the woman pushed. It was a noisy cart, covered in bells and trinkets, which jingled when she went. Around the top, hanging from the roof of the cart like icicles, were hundreds of dreamcatchers, all different sizes, swaying in the breeze and catching the light off their shining stones and crystals.

"Well, rest assured, child, I see you," the old woman followed Isabella's gaze to her cart and smiled wistfully. "The folks around here have little use for my trinkets."

"They're stunning."

"You're too kind." Leaning heavily on a gnarly cane, the woman stood up and tottered over to the cart. Reaching an equal gnarled hand up to the roof of her cart, she pulled down one of the dream catchers. "Here you go, darling. Why don't you have this."

"Oh, I'm not from around here, and I don't have anything to pay you with, but thank you."

The woman laughed warmly, "Don't be ridiculous, dear. I didn't ask for anything in exchange for this. I told you, the people around here have no need for my trinkets, and they're cheap enough for even these fingers to make." She held her hands up as an explanation, fingers as knotted as the trees in the forest around Isabella's house. "A smile from you will be payment enough. Such a young face should not be so melancholy."

Isabella looked at the dreamcatcher in her hands. The outer circle was made of two thin branches intertwined and curved together. The center was wrapped with a mixture of thin leather cord and bright purple and green dyed threads webbed together into two separate smaller circles, open in the center and dotted with turquoise beads. Within each of the open circles were small crystals dangling freely from a thread. Hanging from the outside were three leather tassels, filled with beads and each ending in a delicate feather. The light caught in the crystals, throwing prisms of light across Isabella's face.

"It's beautiful," she said, smiling at the old woman. "But I can't—"

The woman smiled and clucked her tongue. "Payment made, my dear. Payment made." She picked up the handles of her cart and began to wheel it noisily away.

Staring at the dreamcatcher, Isabella felt lighter, less alone. She sighed, releasing some of the pressure that had grown since she trapped herself in this world, and looked at the river. Remembering her brother, Isabella stood up and hurried after the woman. "Wait, miss," she said, rushing across the plaza. "Have you seen my brother?"

"I'm not sure I would know the answer without knowing who your brother was," she smiled at Isabella, but there was a sadness in her eyes this time.

"Of course. He's two years old, blond hair, and the last time I saw him, he was in footed pajamas. His name is Tucker. Has he been through here?"

"I'm not sure if he's been through here," she motioned to the town, "it's a biggish place, and I'm just one woman. But I'm sorry, child, I have not seen him. I do so hope you find him."

"Thank you anyway," Isabella held out her hand to the woman, "I'm Isabella."

She was graced with another warm smile as the old woman accepted the handshake. Isabella felt a slight tingle when their hands touched, "And you can call me Rionach. It is better than what most people call me."

"What do most people call you?"

"Crazy," she winked at Isabella, eyes shining with mischief. Then with a nod, she turned and continued across the plaza, unsuccessfully trying to sell the people her trinkets.

Isabella stood there in the middle of the plaza and watched as Rionach walked away. Putting the dream catcher in her jacket pocket and looking around the plaza, she worried that if Tucker hadn't come through here, this was a waste of time. Finding a way across the river was essential to finding her brother, but there was no bridge here, so Isabella needed to move on, continue her search further down the river. Looking at the carts piled high with food, Isabella realized she hadn't eaten anything for breakfast. Leaving town, she grabbed a purple fruit that looked like a cross between an apple and a strawberry from the cart of a portly man who didn't even acknowledge her presence when she tried to talk to him.

Walking toward the opposite end of town, she tried to figure out how to get through the prickly skin. Distracted, she didn't notice the boy following her until he casually took the fruit from her hand and skipped backward in front of her.

"Hey, I was going to eat that."

"That is what people do," he said as he pulled back his arm and threw it toward the river.

Isabella watched as it tumbled end over end before it plopped into the water. Putting her hands on her hips, she set her jaw and scowled at the boy. He leaned against a tree on the edge of the path, his soft leather boots crossed at the ankles. He wore rough brown pants and a dirty white shirt. His arms were crossed in front of his slender chest, and his head tilted forward and to the right causing his messy brown hair to flop over his right eye. He wore a self-satisfied smile and observed her with a mix of interest and wariness.

"I was going to eat that," Isabella repeated, at a loss for words.

"Yes," he nodded, "you said that already."

"I –"

"Please don't repeat yourself again," he interrupted, "I'm really not all that daft."

"– can't believe you threw my fruit into the river."

"You know you shouldn't deny objective reality," he said, pushing himself off the tree and smirking at her, "and you're welcome."

"I didn't thank you."

"I figured I'd just beat you to the punch," he began to walk down the path in the same direction she was headed, "you're bound to thank me eventually."

"For throwing my breakfast into the river?"

"For saving your life."

Isabella thought for a moment; she didn't actually know what she had taken from the cart, "Was it poisonous?"

"What, the salak fruit? No, it's delicious," he laughed. "You coming?"

"How then did you save my life?" Isabella didn't move, she never liked people who thought so highly of themselves, and this boy was probably one of the most presumptuous kids she'd ever met. His smug smile and carefree attitude got on her nerves immediately.

He stopped and rolled his eyes. Then turning around to grab Isabella's arm and pull her along with him down the way she was initially headed. Isabella pulled her arm away from him, causing him to stumble. He looked at her as if he weren't sure if he should be offended.

"I asked you a question," she planed her feet and stared him down.

"Alright," he said, "you looked like you were on a mission to head somewhere, and I have to report back. I was going to tell you all of this on the way to the river crossing, but we'll do it now."

"You know how to get across the river?"

"One question at a time, but yes," he raised an eyebrow and smiled, clearly enjoying this. "You notice those people in the town back there?" Isabella nodded. "Well, they weren't always so, vanilla."

"Vanilla?"

"Ya, you know, basic, default, vanilla," he shrugged. "Anyway, they slowly stopped interacting with outsiders. At first, we thought it was just isolationism, these hinterlands get like that sometimes, but then some of them started to get this vague, glazed look in their eyes and acted like they didn't even see us. It's weird, right?" He didn't wait for a response before continuing, "Anyway, so they asked me to come here and investigate, and from what I can tell, the more food they eat, the longer people are there, the less they see other people, unless of course they also live in the town, eat the food and such. And so, you're welcome," he stood and held up a finger to stop Isabella from interrupting. "And before you ask, I know you want to get over the river because you are looking for someone because I overheard you telling Rionach about some kid. I'm assuming you want to get over the river because you keep watching it, so either you have some weird thing for water, you're afraid something will climb out of it, or you want to get across. Given you're looking for someone, I'm going with the someone is across the river, and you don't know the way across." He gave a flamboyant bow, then, standing up, smiled, and asked, "How'd I do?"

"I'm not sure whether to be impressed or terrified," Isabella said, her shoulders loosening as she watched his strange monologue.

"I might suggest a little of both," he said, pushing his hair out of his face, "more fun that way. Name's Finnegan, but my friends call me Finn."

"Isabella."

"Cool, can I call you Bella?"

"No," she scrunched her nose, "I'd prefer Izzy. It's what most people call me."

"Izzy it is." He offered his arm, "Shall we?"

"You know the way across the river?"

"Sure do," he said as she walked up next to him, ignoring his offered elbow. He simply shrugged and walked next to her, "I mean, what kind of hunter would I be if I didn't know how to cross a river?" He must have seen the confusion written on her face because he added, "I'll explain on the way."

FOURTEEN

The dirt road that followed the river was barely more than a cart path. Two deep ruts of dry dirt with a smattering of grass between them. Isabella felt like Finn had just been repeating himself for the past seven minutes. She was tired and her feet were sore from the uneven ground. Her stomach was beginning to grumble making her more frustrated with Finn for throwing her food into the river. She had asked him a simply question, and his response was the same as it had been for almost every question she asked.

"Obviously, because I'm a hunter," Finn seemed to think that answered the question because he tried to launch into the next point in his story.

"You can't just repeat the same thing and expect it answers the question," Isabella could hear the frustration in her voice, so she knew it must be clear, but Finn continued, oblivious to her annoyance.

"Seriously, don't you know anything?"

"Excuse me?" She glared at him, "You did not just say that?"

"Well," he stopped and looked at her, "you don't seem to know anything about how things work around here. You clearly haven't heard about the hunters because if you had, you would understand."

Finn had been trying to explain how he'd come to investigate the town where they'd met and how he knew so much about the area. Still, so far, all of his explanations boiled down to being a hunter, which would be fine, Isabella supposed, if he bothered to explain what a hunter was. So far, every time she'd tried to ask about what he was hunting, he chuckled as if it was common knowledge and ignored the question. The only hunters Isabella knew about were the ones that walked around shooting animals, and so far, she hadn't seen a gun on him.

"You mean to tell me," he continued, " you don't know what a hunter is?"

"Yes, that is what I've been trying to tell you this entire time," she rolled her eyes. "You'd think, for someone who claims to be so perceptive, it wouldn't have taken you this long to figure it out."

"But everyone knows," he pushed his hair out of his face again and looked at her with appraising eyes. "Oh no, you're not a Lost One, are you?"

"I am a little lost," she looked around the strange road she was on, the path was dirt, and the trees huddled close by, the ground in between choked with underbrush. "I couldn't tell you where we are if you paid me."

"Why would I pay you for that," he asked with genuine confusion, "I know where I am, I'm a—"

"A hunter, yeh I get it. Do I get to know what a hunter is now?"

"I don't see why not," he sat down on a fallen log and seemed to settle in for a long story.

"While we're walking," Isabella said, pulling him up by his arm, "remember, I'm trying to get across to my brother."

"Right," he said, starting to walk again, "the crossing is just up around the corner," he was quiet for a few steps, then, shaking his head, he continued. "So you really don't know what a hunter is?" Isabella glared at him in response. "Okay, okay," he raised his hands to ward her off, "it's just weird. The hunters are a clan with branches all over the world. We even have a group in the capitol with the council of dreamers, I mean, we haven't gotten a seat on the council, but we're consulted often," he looked at Isabella as if she was supposed to be impressed when she didn't react, he shrugged and went on. "Anyway, we are supposed to keep the denizens safe. You do know who the denizens are, right?"

"Let's pretend I don't."

"Weaver's charms," he said as if it made sense, "do you live under a rock? Okay, so denizens are what the people who live in the towns and the city are called. They live there because the woods aren't always safe, I mean with the shadows and everything."

"Shadows, I know," Isabella jumped with excitement. "I met one of those."

"You m— you what? How are you— Did you— How— what?"

"I met one," she said with a smile and a shrug. "It's the first thing you've said that makes any sense to me at all."

"Let me get this straight, you don't know what hunters are or what denizens are, but you've met a shadow, and you killed it? You are one lucky girl."

"Killed it?" Isabella stopped and grabbed Finn's arm, stopping him and turning him toward her. "Why would I kill it? It showed me where my brother was."

"No, it didn't," he crossed his arms, "not what they do."

"It did," she insisted. "I mean, it took me a long time to get there, so my brother had left, but he'd been there."

"Couldn't have been a shadow," Finn said with certainty, "they attack first and talk never."

"I don't know what else it could have been except a shadow," she said, some of the enthusiasm leaving her voice, "it's the best description I could think of. Weird, dark, kinda translucent, freaky as anything."

"Okay," he said, looking at her with a raised eyebrow, "sounds like a shadow. What did you find when you got where it sent you."

"It was a nice little cottage and a fenced yard, there was this rude talking fox, and then things got weird."

"You met a companion?"

"Is that what you call taking foxes?"

"Any talking animal, really."

"Then I met two," Isabella stood up straighter, looked him in the eyes, and raised both her eyebrows. "I met a white wolf named Vígolfr before the shadow thing came around."

"You are one strange case, Izzy." Finn looked at her with a toothy grin she couldn't help but return. "And we're here."

"Really?" She looked around her, noticing for the first time the path they'd been walking down dove right into the river.

"See the rope there," Finn pointed to a rope strung between two wooden posts on either bank. "We hold that and cross here," he walked toward the river's edge as if walking through a river was the most normal thing in the world.

"What about a bridge?"

He laughed, "Not this far from the capital. Out here, we use the ropes. Just be glad it's a warm day."

Isabella looked up and down the empty river bank; her legs began to feel like rubber, and she felt like throwing up. She watched the water pour past her as she stood on the bank and thought of the news stories about people getting washed away in rivers. Finn grabbed hold of the rope and plunged into the river on the upstream side so the current would push him against it as if it were no big deal. He crossed halfway, holding the rope in front of him, and the water splashed over his shoulders.

"You're not much shorter than me," he called to her over the noise of the water, "you'll be fine."

Isabella walked over to grab the rope. Her arms were shaking as she pictured the current, sweeping her away, and could almost feel the water pushing heavily against her back and overpowering her. As she stood watching the river, her mouth feeling like she was chewing on cotton balls, the water in the river seemed to swell. The sound of water roared in her ears, and the bank seemed to recede into the swells. Rapids appeared where the water had once been calm, and Isabella was rooted on the bank.

She'd never learned to swim, and the thought of being washed down the river, away from her brother, terrified her. She almost didn't hear Finn's grunt as she thought about the water moving too fast for her. She watched him struggle further down the rope, his chest being pushed tight against it. If he couldn't do this, she thought, and he was treating it as nothing, there was no hope for her. The water would be too deep, she thought, too fast. There was no way she'd make it.

"Izzy," Finn's voice sounded choked, "a little help here?"

Isabella looked up but didn't see Finn in the river. Not even the rope was visible. She looked downriver and saw him dangling from the loose end of the rope, pulled down the current now topped with whitecaps. She realized she'd backed away from the rope, and the nearest post was leaning dangerously downstream.

"Finn," she called over the now roaring river, "hold on."

"I'm not planning on letting go if that's what you're afraid of," he sputtered. The current kept pushing his face under, and his hands began slipping toward the rope's frayed end fluttering in the rapids. "Wasn't the plan, anyway."

Isabella tried to get to the stake the rope was attached to, but when she set foot in the water, the river seemed to swell, driving her back to dry land. There wasn't much lying around the bank that could help, but her eyes fell on a large stick. She grabbed it and went down the river until she was even with the boy dangling from the end of the rope. She held onto the branch of a sturdy looking tree and leaned over, holding the stick out over the water.

"Grab this, and I'll pull you in."

Finn reached out with one arm; the hand still holding on began to slip, and he quickly returned the reaching hand to the rope. Hand over hand, he pulled himself back toward the stick.

"Keep going," Isabella called.

"This isn't easy, in case you didn't realize."

"Go past me, then when the river pushed you back, grab the stick on your way by."

Finn nodded in realization and grinned despite the evident struggle to pull himself up the rope. After two more slips, he was just past the branch, and Isabella told him to try again. Reaching out his hand, Finn tried to stretch and reach the stick she held out to him, but as the water pushed him back down the rope, a chunk of wood flew down the river and knocked his arm away from the stick. Their eyes met, panic clear in both sets of eyes.

"The water wheel," Isabella moved farther downstream, grabbing another tree whose roots had recently been exposed as the current carried the river bank away. "Try again, if that thing gives—" She didn't need to finish the sentence for either of them to know the consequences of the water wheel flying down the river.

Once again, Finn let go with one hand, and as he slid down the rope on his one remaining hand, he grabbed for the stick. This time he was able to grab hold. The pressure of the water dragging at him almost pulled Isabella into the river too, but she was able to keep her balance and pull Finn to the shore. Once they had gotten back to the path, safely above the frothing water, they both fell to the ground panting.

"That was close," Finn said, "thanks. Not sure what I'd have done if you hadn't seen the stick."

"How do we get across now," Isabella pushed herself up, hands pushed into the sand behind her. "That rope trick of yours is not going to work."

"Clearly," Finn flopped over on his back and stared up at the clouds floating through the sky. "It's bizarre, though."

"What is?"

"The water," Finn propped himself up on his elbow and looked upriver, "when I went in, it was shallow, like normal. Then it just seemed to kick up out of nowhere. Never seen it do anything like that before."

They sat watching the rapids in the once calm river and the clouds gently floating above them, both of their chests heaving from the exertion, both lost to their thoughts. Finn sat up suddenly and looked upriver again.

"Did you hear that?" He got up and walked to the edge of the water, leaning out to see up the river.

"Hear what?" Isabella stood up and walked to stand next to him.

"It sounded like something big snapped and splashed down into the river," Finn looked downstream then upstream again. "I think people are shouting back in the town. We should probably—"

"Help," the call came from a waterlogged red fox floating on what looked like a broken piece of the water wheel.

Isabella watched as the fox she'd been trapped with floated helplessly down the angry rapids. Her hand went to her mouth, and involuntarily let out a gasp. The fox had been annoying, but it had helped her get out of the trap they'd been in. Albeit she wouldn't have gotten out if it weren't for Isabella either, so she didn't owe her anything. Izzy couldn't stand the thought of anything happening to the poor soft fox, but she also couldn't move. She wracked her brain to try and find something she could do to help.

"Hold on," Finn called out next to her, and without any preamble or probably any plan, took off down the shore of the river, picking his way quickly across the newly exposed roots and disappearing around the corner moments before the fox followed. A loud crack, followed by a large splash up toward the town, drew Isabella's attention back upstream. Bobbing down the river, bouncing off of unseen rocks, the water wheel careened past. Isabella tried to call out a warning, but her breath caught in her throat, and only a desperate choking sound came out as she watched the wheel crash toward the bend after Finn and Kimi.

❧ FIFTEEN ❧

I sabella knew she needed to do something, but she couldn't act the way Finn did. Now wasn't the time for thinking, though, so she didn't have much choice. After seeing the water wheel careen past her through the river, Isabella stopped thinking and started picking a path carefully along the roots; Finn and Kimi would be caught by surprise if the wheel got there first. If she could manage to warn them, everything would work out fine.

Jumping from root to root, Isabella saw the water eating away at the dirt holding the trees in place. The root system became springier with each step, and the water churned further and further under the trunks, washing away more of the dirt that kept them standing on the bank. She would have preferred a better route, but in her rush, she had simply followed Finn's lead, a decision she was now hoping she'd live to regret. The water rose another foot and licked the bottoms of the roots splashing on the top, occasionally making them slippery. Isabella had heard of flash floods before, but she'd never been in one. If this is how they were, she hoped never to be in on again.

Knowing the roots were getting more dangerous, Isabella tried to keep an eye out for a better path. The water wheel had gotten hung up shortly after passing her, so she had been able to get ahead of it. A small lead, but hopefully, it would be enough. Thankful for the rubber soles of her boots, Isabella inched forward carefully on the slippery roots. The water churned beneath her, splashing between the roots. This was not going how she planned, not that she had a plan. The trees groaned as the dirt washed away from underneath them.

The rising water nudged the wheel free of its hang-up, and it spun into the deeper sections of the river, speeding up as it did. Abandoning caution, Isabella leaped from root to root. Twice her left foot slipped off one and into the air above the river, and once, she ran full speed into a branch, knocking the wind out of herself. So, when she reached out to put her foot on what she thought was a root, she was only slightly surprised to realize it was a snake slithering further into the ever more exposed roots, sending Isabella tumbling forward into the raging river.

At the last second, she was able to grab on to one of the newly exposed tree roots. Dangling there in half in the water, the idea of drowning came to her mind again. All thoughts of Finn, Kimi, and the wheel were washed from her mind by the white-capped river's persistent pull. Her only thoughts were getting out and not being pulled under. She struggled to grip the roots, the cold water numbing her fingers as they grappled with the branches. Her boots were torn from her feet, and her sodden jeans made it hard to move her legs. When her hands slipped off the root she was holding for the third time, she flailed for a moment before grabbing a branch dangling low over the water. Her arms ached from the exertion, and she could feel her shoulders burning despite the frigid water.

When the water wheel cracked against the opposite bank, jamming itself against a fallen tree, Isabella remembered why she'd been running in the first place. With renewed purpose, she pulled herself up from the water, using the last of her strength to drag herself onto the roots. She wanted to just lay there forever, but Finn and Kimi were in trouble, and while they both were infuriating, they were also the closest things she had to help in this place. With more effort than should have been necessary, she stood up, balancing on the slippery roots, and she cautiously made her way around the corner.

The scene unfolding before her was not what she expected to see and even seeing it, Isabella wasn't so sure it happened. Finn had shimmied out onto a large tree that had recently fallen over the river. He had his legs wrapped around the trunk of the tree, and he was hanging upside-down, arms outstretched toward the river, while Kimi used her tail to help steer the wood she was floating on so she'd be, more or less, under Finn when she passed by the tree. Finn bit his tongue as he stretched to reach as close to the water as he could. As Kimi's makeshift raft passed below Finn, she leaped up toward his arms.

The wood, freed of her weight, spun out of control and careened down the river toward a second turn.

Finn deftly caught Kimi, and with one swing, she planted her on top of the tree, which she scurried off immediately. Finn, on the other hand, hung back upside-down, then grabbing on with his arms, dangled his legs toward the water. The water wheel dislodged and swept by the river, careened directly toward the tree and Finn.

"Finn," Isabella called out, "look out."
Finn looked over his shoulder at the oncoming water wheel. He swung himself onto the tree, his legs churning as he ran down the trunk toward the shore, jumping as the water wheel crashed into the tree, ripping it from the tenuous hold on the roots and sending both wheel and tree down the river in splinters.

"Thanks, Izzy," Finn said as she caught up to him and Kimi, "heck of a close call." Kimi's red fur was plastered down to her trembling frame, making her look half the size and twice a frail as usual. Finn's hair was drenched and hung into his eyes, dripping unheeded. His shirt was plastered almost transparently to his chest and arms, making Isabella blushed a little when she looked at him.

Kimi glared at Isabella and shook the droplets of water off of her fur, shivered, and curled up in a ball, covering her nose with her tail. She didn't say a word.

"So, what now?"

"Well, we could go see the other hunters," Finn suggested. "It looks like we could all use some dry clothes."

"I need to get to my brother."

"You need boots," Finn gestured at her wet socks. "Besides, they have a boat. Crossing this mess would be a lot easier with a boat, don't you think?"

They agreed to head to the hunter's home, and on the way, Finn continued to explain the world to Isabella. "The hunters are the ones who protect everyone in the world from the shadows," he put a hand up to stall her argument, "I know you think you're friends with one, but believe me, you are not."

Kimi, who joined them, huffed at the statement, but other than the odd sound, she'd been quiet since her rescue.

"Besides the hunters, the Weavers help to get rid of the shadows and take care of the denizens, but you can never count on one being around to help. They're a weird group."

Weavers reminded Isabella of her father's claim to be able to weave dreams, something she'd tried only to trap her brother, and now herself, in a strange and dangerous world. She kept the dreamweaver idea to herself.

"Then there are the wanderers," he glanced over his shoulder at her, "those people just show up, all confused, some talk or interact with others, but for the most part, these people seem catatonic most times. I was beginning to think you were one, but to face down a shadow and live to tell about it— phew, I mean, who knows now."

"Why is facing a shadow so difficult?"

"Well, first of all, most people simply freeze in front of them. Those who don't are more likely to just run away," he shook his head, "until you, I've never heard of someone talking to one of them. You got some backbone, that's for sure."

"Some good it did you at the river," Kimi said, clearly upset about nearly drowning.

"Give her a break," Finn defended her, "can't do much in a raging river."

"You did, Finnegan," Kimi said, not taking her eyes off of Isabella.

"Stop whining. You're fine, aren't you?" Isabella asked, rolling her eyes.

Shifting awkwardly, Finn noted they were almost to the edge of his people's territory. "We're going to have to see the Champion," he said nonchalantly, "I still have to deliver my report, and he'll want to meet you. You are nothing like anyone we've met before.

"I think I'll pass," Kimi said. "I have appointments of my own today."

"Suit yourself," Finn shrugged and pointed down the path; through the woods, Isabella could see the peaks of what looked like tents poking through the underbrush. "Welcome to my home."

Isabella was a little surprised; it seemed the hunters lived in old A-frame tents. She didn't know exactly what to expect, but she knew it wasn't this. In the clearing by the river, the tents looked like something out of a music festival. People moved between them, some having animated conversations.

"Shall we?" This time she took his offered arm.

 SIXTEEN

I s that your camp?" Kimi asked as the area ahead of them hummed with sound and motion.

"Sounds it," Finn said, scratching his head, "but they're normally a lot quieter than this."

"Trouble?" Isabella asked.

He laughed, showing a big-toothed smile to Isabella, "That's not what trouble sounds like. Too much laughing, not enough screaming."

"Why is that not as comforting as I think it was meant to be," Kimi asked. She looked at both of them and shook the last of the water from her fur. "Hunter, thank you for the rescue. At least someone was able to think on their feet," she looked at Isabella with more condescension than a fox should be capable of.

"That's not fair," Isabella stammered, "I-"

"Stood there and watched," Kimi said, "I'll be on my way." Without another word, the fox turned from the hunter's camp toward the woods and bounded into the underbrush.

"That is the rudest, most ungrateful creature ever," Isabella said, crossing her arms and watching Kimi bound into the forest.

"I don't know, Izzy," Finn shook his head, "Kimi is a companion. The fact she hung with us this long, weaver's charms, the fact she even spoke to us is an honor. Companions only truck with weavers, no exceptions." He seemed to think for a moment, then a brightness entered his eyes, and he smirked at her, "You're not a weaver, are you?"

"Do I look like a weaver?"

"Honestly," he shrugged, "no clue. I've never actually seen one. Weavers are rare, like really rare, unless you're near the capitol where they run things, well the council does, but they used to be weavers. They say the weavers used to be shamans in the old world, or their ancestors were. They always travel with their companion, and some can even reshape the world around them to suit their needs. Sure woulda been useful back at the river, right?"

Isabella smiled; his enthusiasm was contagious despite her aching body and sore feet. Since their failed attempts at crossing the river, they had walked farther than Isabella ever had on a single trip her entire life, not to mention the first time she'd gone out for a hike barefoot, she was surprised to even be standing. Finn's boisterous nature and his frequent jokes, though often at the expense of her ignorance, helped to pass the time.

"Don't let this garrulous *mastmaula* fool ya, miss," a deep voice behind them made her jump, "Finn here likes to think he knows a whole lot more than he does."

"Ajay," Finn said, punching the large man in the arm. Finn's hand looking like a baby's compared to the tank of a man who stood before her, "don't be a jerk. You've heard the same stories I have."

"Right," Ajay slapped Finn on the back so hard he stumbled forward, "heard the same stories, believed a lot less of them."

"Okay," Finn bobbed his head and made a face at the man, "you rowdy sheeter."

"Kindly adjust, boy," Ajay's face became serious. "Get on. The Champion is looking for you. You're late."

"Ya, well," Finn motioned at Isabella and smirked.

"Oh no, you don't," she said, pushing him back toward Ajay.

Ajay laughed and grabbed the Finn by his shoulders, steadying him on his feet. "Watch that one, Finn. She's a first-class lady, bound to outdo you, for sure." He winked at Isabella and continued, "Miss, you just tell me if this rumbly muppet is giving you trouble, I'll put the fix on him for you." Then he walked away laughing.

Isabella watched him walk away, "I like him."

"You would," Finn said, "Don't let him fool you. Given my choice, I'd have Ajay at my back any day. Pain in the neck but good in a fight."

"No wonder you get along with him."

"I'll take that as a compliment, Izzy," Finn said and then grabbed her arm and pulled her toward the loudest part of the hunter's camp. "Come on, I wanna show you something. Then I got to get to the Champion. He'll know what's going on."

This part of the camp was not what Isabella had expected it to be. Instead of tents for easy movement, the area looked a lot more like a small town with a main street and side streets. The buildings seemed cobbled together, but they were far more permanent than the simple tents she'd seen earlier. Walking through the camp was like stepping into the past. The wooden buildings leaned together at odd angles, almost defying gravity as they sprouted from the sides of the road. The center, where Finn was currently dragging her, bowed out around a large fountain. The centerpiece of the fountain was a boy standing with his hand out. Water came from his hand and splashed on a dark-robbed figure made of a glossy black stone. Where the water hit the stone, portions of the robbed figure were worn away.

"This," Finn beamed, "is the famed battle of the Champion. The story goes, when he first came from the old world, he faced down a hoard of shadows with nothing more than his bare hands," Finn became louder and more animated as he told the story, and a group of passersby gathered around him listening. "He held his hand out like this and said 'I will not be taken by the likes of you,' then a power came from his hand. They stayed locked in this pose for days, the shadow unable to move, and the Champion never tired. Eventually, the shadow was worn away, and exhausted by the excretion, the Champion collapsed and was found by the local hunter group. The rest is, well, the rest."

"You sure know how to spin a yarn there, Finn," a larger woman said when he was done.

"That boy's been gifted the golden tongue," another onlooker said. "Remember that story he told about facing down three shadows by himself?" The group that had gathered broke up laughing.

Finn scowled. He called after the woman who'd said it. "That happened, Éponine. I'll show you how I beat 'em the next time we spar."

"Good to have you back, Finn," an elderly man leaning heavily on a cane tapped Finn's foot, then moved on, shaking his head and chuckling to himself.

Finn stood there accepting the well-wishes and beaming ear to ear. Here in the camp, she could see how Finn's carefree whimsies affected everyone around him, including her. His infectious smile and laugh were comforting in this strange world. His honest heart clearly won him many loyal friends of all kinds. Maybe he's not the worst person to be traveling with, she thought to herself.

"Finn," another boy about Finn's age ran up and caught him in a bear hug, then pulling back at arm's length, "did you hear?"

"Whoa, Delson, just got back from the field. I don't even know why everyone seems so busy."

"Dude, you didn't hear," Delson was bouncing on the balls of his feet, not even paying any attention to Isabella, "there's a weaver in camp. A real-life weaver."

"What?" Finn's eyes went wide and bright as a crooked smile creased his face. "Here? Where?"

"She's out for recon right now, but they expect her back any minute. She wants us to back her up."

"Back her up with what?"

Delson stopped bouncing and just stared at Finn, "Where have you been, man? Haven't you reported to the Champion yet?" He seemed to notice Isabella for the first time and looked back and forth between her and Finn. "Sorry, didn't see you. Are you from Swift River?"

"Swift River?"

"That's the town we met in," Finn explained. "No, she's from a bit further away."

"Whatever," Delson shrugged, "I gotta go get ready. Find me after you see the Champion." With that, he turned and sprinted across the plaza and down one of the alleys.

"Come on, Izzy, the Champion is this way."

They walked into a long wooden building just opposite the main road they'd traveled to get here. Inside, the walls were more or less ordinary. Some old fashioned weapons hung around the place, but what caught Isabella's attention was the Champion himself. He couldn't have been more than fifteen years old and was not large like Ajay had been. In fact, nothing was intimidating about him.

"Not what I expected," Isabella whispered to Finn as they crossed the long room.

"Looks can be deceiving," was all he said in response.

"Finnegan," the Champion said, his voice fitting his thin frame well, "it's good to have you back, my friend."

"You might change your mind when I tell you what I've found out." Finn continued to explain what he'd found in Swift River. The food was tainted somehow. The more people ate the tainted food, the less they saw the world around them, particularly strangers. He hadn't had a chance to figure out where the contamination came from, but he was at least able to find out where it was happening. When he was done, the Champion sat back and let out a long whistle.

"Seems we have our work cut out for us," he looked at the papers beside him and shuffled a few around, "I'll send Éponine and Hastings to check it out. I have another job for you."

"With respect," Finn interrupted the Champion, who looked taken aback. He didn't seem to be used to having his word questioned. "So," Finn ushered Isabella forward, "I ran into Isabella on her way out of Swift River, and she's looking for her brother, who she says is lost on the other side of the river."

"Get her through at the forge, then get back here."

"See, tried that," Finn flinched a little as he pushed forward. "Problem is, I got halfway across. Izzy was frozen on the bank. I think she's kinda afraid of water." He looked at Isabella and gave her a weak smile, "Good thing though, I got halfway across, and the forge flooded. Almost washed me away, but her quick thinking saved me. As you see, I kinda owe her, so I need to help her find her brother to pay her back."

"Pay me back," Isabella butted in, "for what?"

The Champion answered her, "It is our custom to pay our debts. You saved Finn for us, and we will be eternally grateful. We'd miss this *boloss mec*, 'specially given what's on the horizon. That said, Finn, I'll let you take her across the river, use one of the boats, but then you need to come back here *tout suite*. A weaver has come looking for help. It seems a shadow congress is forming nearby. She needs our help to take it down."

"A shadow congress, I thought they were loners."

"They were," the Champion leaned forward on his knees, "things are changing."

"Got it," Finn turned to leave, "I'll be back as soon as I can. Don't leave without me this time."

Finn stopped by a storefront and talked to the shop keeper; he came out shortly after with two sets of clothes and a pair of boots, one for him and one for her. They were well made, but the fabric was a little rougher than Isabella was used to. Despite that, she was glad to get out of her filthy, wet jeans and into something clean. Isabella looked for a place to change but had to settle for ducking behind the shop. As she pulled on the cloth pants, she was surprised to find them far more comfortable than they looked. Walking back around, Finn grabbed her wet clothes and, without explanation, hung them on a line next to the shop.

"Wait," she said, "not the jacket. I'll hold onto it until it dries."

"Suit yourself," he said, tossing it back to her and shook his head smiling. "A Weaver," Finn seemed in awe, "here. Do you know what that means?"

"You're going to have good clothes?"

"What," Finn rolled his eyes. "Don't tell me you don't know what a weaver is."

"Alright, I won't tell you," she smiled sheepishly at him. She was enjoying how annoyed he got when she didn't know what he thought was simple.

He buried his face in his hands, "Oh weaver's charms, you are daft sometimes."

"And what does that mean? Weaver's charms?"

"It means you know absolutely nothing about the world around you."

"Enlighten me."

"On the way," Finn grabbed her arm and pulled her through the camp.

"Where are you taking me now?" Isabella was tired of walking, and despite the new boots, her feet were killing her, but she let Finn drag her along without too much fight.

"We're going to Nombeko's domain," Finn smiled mischievously at her, "tread lightly there, she's as likely to bite your head off as to help, but she's no match for my charms."

"When do I get to see these charms of yours?" Isabella rolled her eyes, but Finn ignored the comment and launched into an explanation about why he was so excited to see a weaver in the camp, what they did. He even included more details about the stories he'd heard about them, information she took with a grain of salt thanks to Ajay's warning. He also explained how dangerous a single shadow was.

"So a congress of shadows is at least five times as dangerous."

"Because there are five shadows in a congress?"

"No, there's only three. It's five times as dangerous because if they're working together, they are not working on instinct. Most of the shadows we come across are sad creatures who spread misery. It's pathetic, really. But once in a while, you run into one who revels in the negative feelings of others. It's as if some of them are accidents like they never intended to become a shadow, and some seem to relish in the fact. Put three of the latter type together, and you have a trifecta of destruction and desolation."

"So what does this weaver want you to do?"

"Sometimes, when things get too hard for a weaver to take care of on their own, they turn to the hunters, but it hasn't happened for as long as I can remember. So, this is gonna be big." He grinned at her like he was looking forward to the confrontation; Isabella felt a tightening in her chest at the thought of this carefree boy going into battle against the shadows, which she still wasn't convinced were evil.

"I thought you were going to help me?" Isabella asked. "I could use your help finding Tucker, you know this area like the back of your hand. What if I get into trouble again?"

"You're resourceful. You'll figure it out." Finn looked around, his carefree smile faded momentarily, "Look, I know I promised to help you find him, and I will, but I need to do this first. If you can wait until after we take care of the shadow congress, then I'll come with you. I'm just guessing you're not willing to sit around until we're done. I have a duty to my people, one which comes before my promise to help you." His smile came back full force as he added, "I know you understand, right?"

Isabella sighed and scowled at him, trying to show him she did not understand. "Then there's the question of what I do when I find him," Isabella tried to think of anything to convince him. She was trying to appeal to his protectiveness, his cockiness, whatever would keep him from the battle he was so ready to join. "I mean, finding him might prove to be the easy part."

"Just take him back where you're from."

Easier said than done, Isabella thought, "But you could help."

"No Izzy," he stopped and looked at her, all humor had left his eyes, and he looked older than before, "I can't help you, not beyond the river. The Champion gave me permission to do only that. I know you're scared, heck, I wish I could go with you, help look out for you. It's what we do, but this time I cannot. I have a duty to my clan. I swore an oath to protect the denizens and help the weavers. I need to get back and help them. There's no way around that, and please don't ask me to break my word to the hunters. They are my friends, my family, and you do not abandon family. You protect them. I know you understand, or you wouldn't be going through all of this to get to your brother."

"But you promised, you said you were honor-bound to help," Isabella crossed her arms in front of her and raised her eyebrows challenging him to keep his word. She tried to make her voice sound like her parents did when she tried to go back on a promise she hadn't meant to make.

"I did," his shoulders sunk under her gaze, and he sighed, "but I also made a promise to my people, and right now that promise takes priority. I'm sorry, but the way I see it, I'm not breaking my promise to you, just delaying it. I'll give you what help I can now, get you over the river, and when all this is over, I'll come find you to see if you need more, but hopefully, you'll have your brother and be gone by then. You have to remember to know who to trust, somethings can be very manipulative," he looked at Isabella and set his jaw. "We'll take the boat to the landing just upstream together, but once we're there, I'm turning around and returning to my honor-bound duty. It's the right thing to do."

❧SEVENTEEN❧

I sabella and Finn's conversation had died after he'd declared he would not help her beyond the river. While Isabella realized she should be grateful for the help he is giving her, she still felt abandoned by him at the same time. He claimed to be someone who helped wanderers or denizens or whoever these people were, people who were struggling to survive in this strange world, but here she was, struggling to rescue her brother from this all too realistic dream, and he refused to help her. She was thinking about this disparity, getting increasingly frustrated with him and herself, when they arrived at the hunter camp's quartermaster.

Of all the buildings in this makeshift camp, which Isabella still viewed as more of a town than a camp, this building looks the least likely to be dismantled and put back up elsewhere. The quartermaster's structure was made out of sturdy wood, with large beams crisscrossing through the ceiling. Every inch of the cramped wall space was covered with supplies. Weapons were mixed in with climbing gear, general household items, and farming equipment. There didn't seem to be any structure or organization for the placement of things, except maybe they were just put where there happened to be room.

The quartermaster herself was a stout woman with dark skin and thick limbs. Her black hair was close-cropped and curly, and she stomped around the room like she was trying to test the soundness of the floorboards. Finn argued with the woman for a while about getting things for their short journey; Isabella, in a combination of annoyance and boredom, decided to let him deal with it alone and wandered outside to watch the general bustle around the camp.

The people who lived here were more diverse than Isabella had ever seen in one place. Where she lived, most of the people were descended from northern or central Europe. There were a few African-American or Middle Eastern kids in her school, but she could count them probably on one hand. Here she saw people of all nationalities. It was staggering at first, but the seamlessness of their interactions, the banter between groups of people walking around, made the physical differences seem less stark, less obvious.

"One of the best camps," Isabella jumped as a voice beside her broke her reverie. Looking over, she saw a woman, probably in her late twenties leaning next to her on the wall of the quartermaster's house. She wore a bright orange sweater with a picture of a gray cat in a playful pounce pose. The shoulders and forearms of the sweater were reinforced with stiff leather pads, making the shirt seem awkward. Her pants were made of tight leather material, similar to what adorned her shoulders, but dark black. Around her waist were a collection of small throwing knives and two larger knives in sheaves on her back, the handles sticking down behind each of her arms. She must have noticed Isabella's surprise because she immediately continued, "I'm sorry, I didn't mean to startle you. I was just commenting on how well the Champion runs this camp. I'm Wren. It's nice to meet you." She stuck her hand out toward Isabella and smiled warmly.

"It's alright," Isabella stammered, accepting the handshake, "I just didn't hear you come up."

"I'm surprised at that," she said, resting her right foot against the wall and crossing her arms in front of herself, "you hunters normally have such good instincts for things like that."

"I'm not a hunter."

"My mistake," she says, expectantly scanning the sky. "I just figured, given your outfit and where we are and all."

"Right," Isabella flushed with embarrassment, "my clothes were soaked from trying to cross the river, then Finn brought me here and gave me these to put on."

"Finn?"

"He's one of the hunters." She motioned toward the door of the quartermasters, "He's in there trying to get some stuff to help us get across the river."

"Nombeko is hard to impress." Wren didn't elaborate; instead, she kept watching the skies expectantly. The two stood in companionable silence for a while, then Isabella, struck by the absurdity of her present situation, rubbed her eyes and chuckled. Wren broke her skyward gaze and looked at Isabella inquisitively. "Everything alright?"

"Yeah," she said, regaining her composure. "I was just struck by how absurd all of this is."

"All of what?"

"This," she motioned to the camp around her. "All of this."

"I don't understand?" Wren pushed off from the wall and turned to face Isabella, she was an imposing woman, but Isabella smiled because, despite the leather and the knives, Wren was wearing this ridiculous sweater. "These hunters are getting ready for a major offensive against a shadow congress. It's nothing to laugh at. Some of these fine warriors will be giving their lives to help lessen the threat haunting these lands." Seeing Isabella's smile, Wren put her hands on her hips and scowled at her, "Have some respect, young lady. Don't you understand what's at stake here?"

"That's just it," Isabella couldn't help to feel intimidated in the presence of Wren, but the senselessness of the intimidation made her smile, "you would think I would– understand what's at stake like you said. I mean, I made this place. This is my dream, but I'm being pushed through it like some leaf in a stream. Of course, right now, it seems more like a river. All I want to do is find my brother and get him home to our parents."

Wren's demeanor didn't slacken for a moment during Isabella's explanation. In fact, it became more abrasive as she asked, "You *made* this place?"

"I must have, right? It's my dream," Isabella figured there was no harm in explaining everything to her subconscious. Maybe it would help her to break down the problem and get to her brother quicker. "You see, my brother was being annoying, so I wove him this dream like my dad does for me when I'm having nightmares. Only it seems I did it wrong, and I trapped him in his dream."

"Trapped him?" Wren's posture had relaxed a bit during the explanation, and Isabella took the change which came over Wren as a good sign and kept going.

"He disappeared from our bedroom. He's only two, so it's not like he climbed out of his crib and ran away. Mom has the police out looking for him, but I know he's in here. I've actually seen him a few times, but he's always out of my reach, or something stops me. This shadowy figure showed me this place in a frozen lake and showed my brother by the river, so I put myself here in my dream. This is all just the creation of my subconscious mind, so none of it matters except getting my brother."

"A shadow told you about this place?"

"He was nice, actually. He showed my brother at the cottage."

"So why didn't you just dream of the cottage and get your brother out of your subconscious?" Something about the tone of Wren's voice made Isabella think she was just humoring her.

"I did," Isabella shrugged her shoulders, "but I guess it was some sort of dream trap. So when we got out of that, I ended up wandering into this strange town where I met up with Finn."

"We?"

"What?"

"You said we when you were talking about getting out of the dream trap."

"Right," Isabella rolled her eyes, "there was this annoying talking fox there, but the shadow had warned me not to trust it, so I was able to get out despite its best efforts. It's all a little unnerving because it seems to have been following me."

"Now I get it," Wren said with a smile. Another glance at the sky and a broad smile lit up her face. From out of the clouds came a large hawk which swooped down toward them. Isabella flinched, covering her face with her hands to ward off the sharp talons obviously descending on her. "Relax, this is Mentu, my companion."

"Finn said something about companions before," Isabella tentatively lowered her arm and looked at the hawk, now perched on Wren's shoulders, watching her warily, "what are they?"

"Companions are animal companions to dreamweavers when they're in the dream world. Each dreamweaver's companion is unique and represents a valuable, albeit often overlooked, part of their personality. Mentu here is my companion when he deigns to come down from his lofty world to stand with us mere mortals."

"Really, Wren," the voice from the hawk on her shoulder surprised Isabella with its calm and cultured tone, "do you have to be so melodramatic."

"I'm just picking on ya Mentu," she said, winking at Isabella, "don't get your feathers all ruffled."

Mentu ruffled his feathers, causing several to get into Wren's face. Smiling as she pushed the feathers away from her face, "Don't be a jerk."

"You did ask for it," Mentu said, and then began to preen himself.

Wren shifted her attention back to Isabella, "I'm still trying to figure out what part of my personality Mentu is supposed to represent, but I'm beginning to think it's not one of my better attributes."

"I should let you know," Mentu said, lifting his beak from under his wing, "your counterpart is on his way."

"Counterpart?"

"Usually," Wren explained, "Weavers work alone."

Mentu stopped preening again and glared at Wren.

"Oh, you old fuss," she rolled her eyes, "you know what I meant." Mentu ruffled his feathers in response before going back to preening himself. "Normally, weavers only work with their companions," she looked at Mentu, who nodded his approval. "Anyway, this being a shadow congress, I called my old trainer in to help. I try not to use him for these longer missions with his family and all, but this was important."

"I don't like his dog," Mentu said between smoothing out his tail. "The shaggy thing gives me the creeps."

"Cut them some slack, pretty boy," Wren chuckled, "those two fight the terrors. They need to be slightly terrifying themselves. Besides, it's not a dog, the thing's a—"

"You said things made sense when I told you what was going on?" Isabella interrupted; she enjoyed the banter between Mentu and Wren, but it wasn't going to help her get her brother back.

"Right," Wren said, refocusing her attention on Isabella. Wren examined her with a critical eye, and she didn't say anything else for a while. Isabell was about to say something when Wren began. "As far as I can tell, you are either a Walker or a Weaver. You just haven't come into your own yet, which isn't surprising. Most dreamweavers don't come into their own until early adulthood, and by the looks of you, you're what twelve?"

"Fourteen," Isabella furrowed her brow at Wren. "I'm small for my age."

"Either way," she continued, "not early adulthood, so you're a little premature. Dream Walkers come into their own even later. I've heard of a few cases where a child of a dreamweaver who come from some of the older families start as early as seventeen, but fourteen seems a bit off. Anyway, if you're a Weaver, this fox you mentioned is probably your companion. Walkers don't have companions like that."

"All this about Weavers and Walkers, companions, hunters and denizens, none of it makes sense," Isabella rolled her eyes and shook her head. She felt lost in this place, which frustrated her more because it was her dream.

"It's not that hard," Wren shrugged, "let me explain."

"Wren," Mentu ruffled his feathers, shifting uneasily from one foot to the other.

"Oh relax, the rules are to keep us from explaining everything to the hunters and the denizens, weavers and walkers, they get to know."

"But if she isn't—"

"Then the council will get mad at me again," when Wren smiled, there was a bit of a gleam in her eyes, "won't be the last time."

"But they said—"

"Are you going to tell them?" At that, Mentu ruffled his feathers again and went back to preening. "He worries too much," Wren sighed. "Anyway, weavers, or dreamweavers, are people like me. Our job, when we're here, is to protect the dreamers and denizens from the shadows and the stalkers."

"Dreamers?"

"People who are dreaming, they wander aimlessly in here, seeing what their subconscious wants them to. The shadows hunt them, and while most can get away, some need our help."

"What if no one's there to help them?"

"Then the shadows take them," Wren's shoulders slumped, and she bowed her head slightly before she went on, "they become part of this world."

"This world?"

"The dream world; they become denizens or hunters or —" when she looked up at Isabella, her eyes glistened in the sun, "—or shadows themselves. All depends on how they see themselves. Weavers and Walkers help those who need it beat the shadows if we can protect those who can't protect themselves. Difference is, Walkers either never found their companions or lost them somehow."

"Lost them?"

"If a Weaver loses their companion," she glanced at Mentu and smiled warmly, "one of two things will happen. They will either become a Walker or a Stalker. Walkers are never fully settled, tend to be reckless, and seem incomplete somehow. They become weaker than they were with their companion."

"So what's a Stalker?"

"Dream Stalkers are the dark side of the Walkers. They work with the shadows or for them, I'm not sure which, but the end result is the same. Where we try and help the dreamers, Stalkers do the opposite, I've met a few in my time, and they are powerful. When they work with the shadows, which are normally aimless wanderers and loners, they create the terrors."

"Like what your counterpart fights?"

"Exactly," Wren nodded. "So, the way I see it, the fox you told me about, she could be your companion, but why you made contact so early, I couldn't say."

"No way," Isabella responded. "I was warned about her. She was trying to stop me from getting my brother."

"The shadow told you that?" Wren shook her head. "Doesn't matter, you can just drop that line at the door. Shadows are bad business."

"But that fox, her name was Kimi I think, tried to trap me in the house thing." Isabella clarified, gaining a nod from Wren. "She tried to keep me from getting to my brother."

"Again, I'm going with no," she held her hand up to Isabella to stop her from interrupting. "That trap was probably the shadow trying to get to you. The fox told you her name too, I see," she raised her eyebrows at Mentu, who preened his feathers on her shoulder pretending not to notice. "The reason Kimi was there was probably to help you get out of the trap. Think about it carefully. Was your brother at the house when you got there? Was Kimi trying to get you to go deeper into the trap or to get out of it? As for the whole keeping you from your brother, I wasn't there, so I'm not going to talk about that, but if I had to put money on it, I'd say you didn't understand what she was trying to get you to do.

"I have to get going to meet with some of the hunters," she started to leave but turned back, "If you think about it, you are here, now. You ran into me to explain all of this. Finn and his people are helping you get to your brother. Seems to me you're better off now than you were when you started. If I'm right, and I usually am, foxes aren't solitary creatures. They live in packs or families, they hunt together, they play together. They are stronger together than they are alone. Keep that in mind.

"And one more thing, this is not your subconscious. Dreams never were, here the rules are different, the stakes are different, but it is no less of a real-world than the waking world. If you are a weaver, and I suspect you are, then you'll learn soon enough. Good luck, Isabella, and try to give Kimi another chance." Wren waved and turned to leave, calling back over her shoulder, "Oh ya, and tell Finn I was sorry I missed him; I've heard some impressing stories about him from the other hunters here."

"Wait," Isabella called after Wren, "rules, stakes? What are you talking about?"

"You'll find out," she said without turning around.

Isabella watched as Wren walked across the plaza toward the Champion's house. Her mind swirled with what the woman with the hawk had said. If this was a different world, a different dimension, then more could be at stake for her brother than she initially thought. If he wanders into the area the shadow had shown her, the grove with the withered trees, then he'd be trapped here. She wanted to run after the woman, but something told her Wren had bigger problems to deal with. The idea of the shadow congress seems more ominous after talking with her.

"Score," Finn said, bursting out of the Nombeko's place. Isabella turned to look at him, and he stopped short, raising his eyebrows, "Izzy, you alright? You look like someone has walked over your grave."

"I met the Weaver," Isabella looked at the collection of stuff piled in Finn's arms with renewed trepidation, "she said 'Hi.'"

"What?" Finn craned his neck around Isabella to try and catch a glimpse of the woman with the hawk, but she had already gone inside the Champion's house. "That's not fair. I always wanted to meet a weaver. I always miss the cool stuff," he winked. "What was she like? Did you meet her companion? I hear she's as tough as they come." He kept firing off questions too fast to answer, but it was just as well because Isabella was too busy thinking about what Wren had told her about dreamweavers. "Izzy," Finn waved a free hand in front of Isabella's face, "you in there? What did she say to make you go all pale like this? I mean, it looks like you're about to pass out? Seriously, what did she tell you?"

"She said–" Isabella started, but then the absurdity of what she was going to say stopped her tongue and changed her mind. "Doesn't matter. We have to get going. What's all this stuff for?"

"Just wait 'till I tell you," Finn had his customary toothy grin on as he stated, handing Isabella an assortment of treasures he'd wrangled from Nombeko's domain.

EIGHTEEN

This thing doesn't make any sense," Isabella complained as she tried to nock an arrow on the bow Finn had given her. "Why do I need this stupid thing anyway?"

"I figured with the shadow congress and all– now watch," Finn shrugged, showing her for the fifth time how to properly nock an arrow. "I've been using a bow for as long as I can remember. You can get it."

"Says you," Isabella held the bow in her left hand, pointed down to the ground. She took an arrow from the quiver leaning against a tree and examined it. The nock at the back looked simple enough, but every time it was set just below the nock point, the arrow would angle away from the bow. The couple she did manage to shoot flew wildly to the right or left. "Am I even holding this right?"

"You said you write with your right hand, so you hold the bow in your left."

"But I throw with my left hand when I play softball."

"Not sure what softball is," Finn said, dismissing Isabella's question, "but there's nothing soft about archery." Finn paused for a second, grinning expectantly at Isabella for a moment in silence before he continued. "You know," he said, beginning to chuckle at his joke, "because archery is hard. Get it."

Isabella narrowed her eyes at him and bit her lip before she said, "Not. Funny."

Each arrow Finn shot flew straight from his bow and lodged into his target. Isabella's would seem to drip from the bow and embed themselves in the grass mere feet in front of her. She grunted in frustration and threw both the bow and the arrow to the ground, stomping away.

"Let me go through it again–"

"We've been through it five times already Finn," Isabella crossed her arms in front of her chest. "There is just no point. Besides, I don't see why I need this."

"You need to be able to protect yourself against the –"

"The shadows," she mimicked him. "Yes, I know you think that, but we've been at this all day. The sun is almost down, and I need to find my brother. I've talked to one of your shadows. They're not actually all bad. I mean, have you ever tried to –"

"Talk to them," Finn rolled his eyes and let out a sigh. "What you don't seem to realize is they don't like to talk. What you experienced is not the norm with shadows. They attack first and talk like never. These things are pure evil, so don't try to pretend you know this place better than I do. I mean, yesterday, you didn't even know what a Weaver was." He bent down and picked up her bow. "Now take this thing, and we will go over this for the sixth time, and the tenth time, and the 30th time if that's what it takes for you to figure it out." He held the bow out to her, staring through bright green eyes under a mop of brown hair. They stood there in stubborn silence until Isabella dropped her shoulders and walked up to take the bow from Finn.

"Fine," she retorted, "but don't say I didn't warn you when a rogue arrow flies at you."

"I'll be fine," Finn grabbed her arms and dragged her toward him and putting her arms where they needed to go. He helped her draw back, keeping the arrow tight to the bow. "Alright," he said, his breath against her ear made her flush, "now breathe slowly, and let go." The arrow flew over the field and lodged itself into the tree on the other side of the clearing. "See, I told you you could do it."

"With your help," she said, "but you're not coming to help." She felt guilty for nudging him as soon as the words left her mouth. "I'm sorry," she said to the top of his bowed head, "that was mean."

"A little bit."

"Hold on, I'll get the arrow," she said, happy to be out of the embarrassing situation at least for a couple of minutes.

Walking across the field, Isabella considered the road ahead of her. She liked having Finn with her; he always seemed to know what to do, he never froze like she would, but she understood now why he couldn't come. Wren had made it completely clear, and Isabella admired Finn's loyalty to his friends; still, having him along would make things easier. She needed to save her brother, rescue him from where she put him. Now, she would need to finish alone.

As she struggled to get the arrow out of the tree, Isabella saw something moving in the shadows of the forest, and she froze. She could hear Finn going through their supplies on the other side of the field they were using for her impromptu lesson, but calling for him would definitely alert whatever was in the woods to her presence. If she could get the arrow quietly and get back to him, then he'd be able to take care of it for her. Isabella grasped the shaft of the arrow and, twisting it slightly as Finn had shown her, pulled it out of the tree. The rustling in the trees grew closer, and as she looked back toward Finn searching through his backpack for something, the realization she couldn't rely on him to help her in every dangerous situation seemed to slam down on her. He was getting ready to go off with Wren to fight her shadow congress; by comparison, Isabella's problems were small.

Taking a deep breath, Isabella held the arrow, point down like she'd seen people do with knives in movies, then bending her knees, so she was lower to the ground, she moved toward the sound and away from the relative safety of Finn's company. When she approached the edge of the woods, twilight had begun to stretch its legs through the deeper parts of the woods already, and she had to squint to see. Something moved deeper in the woods; a flash of color behind a tree off to her left caught her eye. Sinking to her knees to get a better view, Isabella leaned into the undergrowth, careful not to move the rustling branches.

"What do you see?" Finn's voice over her right shoulder made Isabella jump and squeak in surprise.

"You jerk," she said, pushing him, "you scared me."

By his toothy smile, it was clear he was proud of himself. He laughed and stood up, extending his hand to help Isabella off the ground. She took it, but once she was standing, she pushed him, smiling herself as the initial scare wore off. He put up his hands in mock defense and laughed again.

"For your information," Isabella put her hands on her hips, half scolding him, half keeping herself from laughing, "I saw something moving out there in the woods and wanted to make sure it wasn't anything following us."

"Ahh, got it. And?"

"And you scared it away before I had a chance to find out."

"You know that's not how you use one of those," he pointed to the arrow, barely able to restrain his smile.

Isabella looked at the arrow still clutched in his hand. She narrowed her eyes at him and took a deep breath, reminding herself he was just trying to be funny and willing herself to ignore his comment. Instead, she looked back into the woods, "I wonder what was out there."

"It's Kimi."

"Where?" Isabella looked around. She hadn't seen the fox since before they entered the hunter's camp, and she was beginning to miss her.

"Out in the woods," he turned to walk back to their supplies. "I'm impressed you even spotted her. She's good. Been following us ever since we left the camp, I figured she'd come say hi when she wanted to."

"Why didn't you say anything," Isabella asked into the woods, then turned when she didn't get an answer and jogged to catch back up to Finn, "Why didn't you tell me?"

"You hadn't seemed very interested in her before," he shrugged, "plus, you said it was her fault you were in the trap. Just figured you didn't care. She's interested in you, though, for whatever reason. But come on, it's going to be dark soon, and we should be at the landing before night. I hate being in the middle of nowhere. The shadows are strongest in the moonlight."

"What do you mean strongest?"

"Well, shadows don't typically come out much in the sunlight, they will occasionally, but they are never as strong or as dangerous. Plus, in daylight, they're easy to avoid. They stick mostly to the shady areas in the trees, so all we do is stick to the field when we can. At night, well, that's kinda their time."

"But what about Tucker?"

"Let's hope he can avoid running into a shadow," Finn waved the question off, preoccupied with repacking the bags after their impromptu training session. "He's a visitor, shadows love them, but it rarely works out too well for the visitor."

Isabella felt her heart drop as she listened to Finn. A new wave of panic surfaced, and she looked around as if fenced in on all sides by lurking shadows. Her brother was wandering through the woods alone, unaware of the danger he was in. She didn't care so much that she was in danger now, too; it was a penance for sending her brother away. Her brother hadn't done anything wrong; she was just tired of him waking her up and wanted to get a good night's sleep. Now, she realized, he was probably being hunted by the same shadows which haunted his dreams every night, only this wasn't a dream. He was in their world, a place where the things that went bump in the night could actually hurt him.

"We have to hurry, Finn," Isabella was spurred on by a new sense of urgency. "I didn't realize how much danger I put him in by sending him here."

"You didn't send him here," Finn's dismissiveness annoyed her, "only Weavers like Wren or Stalkers send people here. You're not a Weaver, and Wren would never have let you leave the camp if you were a Stalker. Weavers hate them."

"How do you know I'm not a Weaver?" Isabella thought about what Wren had told her.

"Easy," Finn said, smiling back to her, "you wouldn't hate Kimi so much if you were. Weavers are drawn to their companions. Stalkers don't have them or have driven them away, I guess, bad news either way. You're probably just a visitor, like your brother," he stopped suddenly and looked up at her. "Do not tell Nombeko. Hunters don't give visitors supplies. We never get them back. I convinced her you were another hunter on a mission from a different clan and had lost your supplies in the river. She'd kill me if she knew I was giving stuff to a visitor."

"Why are you helping me, then?"

"Not sure really," Finn said, shouldering his pack and holding the other out for her, "just seemed like the right thing to do."

They walked the rest of the way to the landing in relative quiet. As night fell around them, slinking out of the trees like a cat hunting its prey, Finn visibly tensed and walked with an arrow constantly nocked. He moved like a hunter should, Isabella noticed, like he belongs on a forest's trails. She tried to imagine him in any other setting, walking the streets of a city or going to class at school, none of it fit. Here he was home, he belonged, and for the first time, she wondered how he came to live in the dream world.

They reached the landing late at night and had to knock on the boat keeper's door. He came out, an impossibly thin man with a long grey beard. He wanted them to wait until morning, warning the waters were always rougher at night, but Isabella was insistent, and Finn was persuasive. In the end, they were loading their supplies into a small canoe not long after they reached the landing.

"It'll probably be about ten minutes to cross here," Finn said as he collected the oars from beside the boathouse. "I'll get you settled over on the other side, then you'll just need to travel back down the river the way we came to get to where your brother was. You should see Swift River sometime around dawn if you move quick."

"Tucker's got to go through the whole night by himself?"

"Unless you know a quicker way to travel," he said, shaking his head, "I've heard some Weavers near the capital have figured out how to fly."

"Your misconceptions about Weavers are probably the most absurd things I've ever heard," a quiet voice from the shadows startled both of them, and they turned quickly, Finn's hand dropped to the bow on the ground next to him.

Isabella searched the shadows in vain to find the speaker. Her bow was stowed in the canoe, and not wanting to take her eyes from the shadows, she searched the ground for some way to defend herself. Keeping her eyes on the edge of the woods, scanning the tree trunks for the speaker. Her hand fell on a smooth, cool, pointed piece of metal sitting on the sand by the water's edge. Moving her fingers down the metal, she felt a rigid wooden handle, and sparing a glance, her fingers rested on a small fishing knife, presumable forgotten after someone's day trying to catch dinner in the river. The thought made her stomach rumble, realizing she hadn't eaten since coming here.

"Show yourself," Finn's voice was commanding, "we're armed and don't like surprises."

"Now Finn," the voice said, the edge of a laugh clear in its tone, "is that any way to treat an old friend?"

"If you're a friend," Isabella said, grasping the handle of the knife with white knuckles, "then come on out and say hi."

"You have made it clear I am not your friend, Isabella," the laughter left the voice, "but out of duty to my brother, I will help you none the less. Whether you want me to or not."

Isabella's mind raced back to Vígolfr, the arctic wolf she'd met on the frozen lake, he'd mentioned his sister was coming to help, but Isabella didn't remember ever seeing her. "Are you Vígolfr's sister?" She asked the darkness of the forest, "He said you'd be coming to help."

"And I have," the voice continued, "and been spurned for it, but here I am. I will see you through this like I promised my brother, but once I have, and you are gone, I'm sure our paths will never cross again." With that, a sleek red fox walked out of the undergrowth, tail and head held high, and stood on the moonlit bank.

Immediately, Finn drops his bow, "Kimi," he calls out in excitement, "I was wondering when you'd show yourself. You almost missed the boat."

"I considered it," she looked at the clear expression of shock on Isabella's face, "I truly considered it."

"But you're not a wolf," Isabella tried to make sense of the conversation with Vígolfr, tried to see if she missed something.

"Astute as always, Izzy," Finn flashed her a toothy grin, which faded when he saw the confusion and concern on her face.

"He said his sister was coming."

"In those of honor and virtue, family is not determined by our blood, but by our loyalty," Kimi said, looking with sadness on Isabella, "I figured your time with Finn would have shown you that."

Isabella looked between Finn, who had gone back to packing the canoe, and Kimi, who had moved closer to the canoe. Neither said anything more as they finished getting ready.

Eventually, the shock wore off from Isabella, and she tried to reassess everything she'd experienced. Wren told her Kimi had probably tried to help, but Isabella's experience at the cottage didn't come close to what she would consider help. Kimi didn't care about her brother then. Why would she care now? Isabella wrestled with the question as the three of them loaded into the canoe and set out across the choppy water, which once again seemed to swell, trying to swallow her up as she got closer.

 NINETEEN

The canoe's prow slammed down on another white cap as they crossed the river, jarring her in her seat. Isabella and her father had canoed before, but it was nothing like this, and she always wore a life vest. When she'd asked Finn about them, he looked at her like he didn't understand, handed her a paddle, and told her to help launch the boat.

Finn had opted for the back, which was just as well because Isabella knew she was terrible at steering in calm waters, and this was anything but calm. Another jarring wave caused Kimi to whimper as she hunkered down in the middle of the canoe. Given her previous experience in a river, she had expressed her displeasure at crossing the water, but Isabella knew it was the only way to get to her brother, and nothing was going to keep her from him.

"Dig the paddle in deeper," Finn yelled over the roar of the water. "I've never seen the waters like this before. I've heard stories but never seen it. We need to get past these rapids. I see some calmer water up ahead."

Isabella wiped the water from her face, "I'm doing the best I can."

"Lean into it more," the current was pushing them back toward the shore they'd launched from, twisting them sidewise, buffeting them, coming close to swamping them several times already, and they hadn't been on the water for a full minute yet. Finn had said ten minutes to cross, but Izzy was sure it would be longer at this rate.

"I'm trying," the current twisted them once more, bringing the gunnel of the boat almost level with the water. Isabella leaned to the other side, trying to balance out against the constantly changing currents. "Can you keep this thing going in a straight line?"

"Nope," he yelled, and she could swear he was laughing, but she didn't want to risk the look back.

In the base of the canoe, drenched from the seemingly eager river trying to swallow their little boat, Kimi huddled in between the seats, whimpering each time the waves hit. "Let's just go back," she said weakly, "I changed my mind."

"We are not going back," Isabella scolded her. "No one asked you to come along anyway, and we are not going to abandon my brother because you don't like getting wet."

"Says the girl who would've let me drown yesterday."

"Will you two stop bickering and help me get this thing out of the waves so we can get across?" Finn sounded like he was straining, and the boat started to point toward the opposite shore once more.

"What can I do," Kimi whined, "it's not like I can row this thing."

"Paddle," Isabella corrected her, "this is a canoe. You row a boat."

"No, I don't," Kimi snapped back. "I hunt mice. I dig dens. I do not *paddle* boats."

"But you can see in the dark," Finn called as they got sideswiped by another wave threatening to capsize their canoe. "Keep an eye out for waves, and I can try to turn into them. We'll make better headway."

Kimi grumbled, but she put her front paws on the edge of the canoe so she could see out. Each time she called out a wave, Finn would turn the boat upstream and meet it with the bow. Each time the water would splash over the bow, drenching Isabella again and again, but they were making more progress, so she didn't complain. They were getting into a working pattern: paddle, call, turn, paddle, paddle, call, turn, paddle. The heavy weight of failure she'd felt ever since the first experience with the river started to lift and Isabella was beginning to think they might actually make it across in one piece.

"What's that?" Kimi asked, leaning over the side when the waves had calmed down at one point.

"Another wave?" Finn asked, beginning to turn the canoe into the current. Isabella couldn't see the wave, though she had been getting good at spotting them after about five minutes.

"No, no," Kimi said, "it's something else." She leaned further over the edge, trying to get closer and a better look.

"Careful you don't fall in," Isabella warned when the weight of the little fox began to sway the balance of the boat.

"Something is floating in the water out there," Kimi said, ignoring the warning and leaning further over the edge.

"What do you see, Kimi?" Finn asked, turning the boat back across to make up some distance while the water was calm.

"It looks like a person," Kimi was leaning over the edge so far Isabella leaned in the opposite direction to balance out the boat in case a wave came.

Thoughts of her brother being washed away while playing on the bank of the river came to her mind. "We need to see who it is," Isabella said, scared it could be her brother or someone like him who needed help. The thought of anyone struggle through these waters terrified her. Finn steered the canoe upstream, and they dug deep into the water, making minimal headway against the current.

"It's still too far away to make it out," Kimi said.

"You sure it's a person?" Finn asked, "I'd be surprised anyone would try to swim this tonight."

"People swim this?" Isabella was surprised anyone would want to swim this in the day time, nonetheless at night.

"Sure," Finn said, "it's not usually this strong. Must be the flash flood we got caught in upriver still messing things up."

"Oh, weaver's charms," Kimi called out, rearing back on her hind legs in the canoe. "Turn back Finn, it's a shadow."

"On the water?" Finn called out frantically, trying to turn the canoe away from the shadow now menacing the port side. The current picked up again. Kimi jumped to the starboard. Isabella, already overbalanced after Kimi's sudden shift, slipped and fumbled her paddle. It spun out of her hands into Kimi's stomach, pushing both of them further starboard. The canoe heeled until the river threatened to swamp them. The paddle continued to spin off Kimi, and Finn swatted it away into the water. When the paddle splashed into the water, the boat rocked violently upstream. Downstream, the water bulged as something from the depths rushed to the surface, and Isabella lost her footing.

The light of the moon was blotted out and watery. Isabella could hear shouting, but it sounded far away, but under the warm covers of her bed, in the safety of her room, none of it made sense. She pulled the covers up tighter around her and could feel the warm hug of oblivion pressing down on her. Voices above her still called out her name, muffled against the blankets pulled over her head. There was a comfort for her, sinking in the warmth of sleep. The sound of her mother calling her to bed, singing to her, *Too ra loo ra loo ra*. She wanted to keep sinking into the comforts of sleep. The voices above her sounded urgent, and she heard splashing as a hand grab her from above. She resisted, sinking deeper into the welcoming darkness.

When her head broke the top of the water, Isabella gasped, her eyes shooting open. Her lungs burned, and she wanted to go back to bed. She swatted the hand pulling her away from her mother's embrace. "Stop," she cried, "I want to go back to bed." Isabella writhed out of the grasp and back into the pull of oblivion. Images flashed before her eyes, her father rocking her, kissing her good night. Her mother's lips, singing her old lullabies. Her brother, Tucker, laughing as she tickled him, the life and joy glistening his eyes. Then more images, darker images. Her mother's tears, crying for the loss of her child, her children. Her father standing in the rain, looking up at the sky, water streaming down his face. Tucker, sitting on the edge of a sandbox, his little hands covering his eyes, hiding from something, his breaths come in hitching sobs. Again the arm pulled at her, drawing her toward a hard light she didn't want to see. It was warm where she was, cozy under the covers. She felt safe here.

Another splash and the water washed around her head; she flailed, her eyes closed against the burning. She fought the hands threatening to pull her from sleep, from warmth, from her mother, into the darkness. She wanted to sleep more, enjoyed the comforting pressure, the hug rocking her smoothly to sleep.

Then there was pain, and with the pain came the cold and the wet. She coughed and sputtered half in the water, half dangling in the air. Her senses muddled, swaying in and out, but the pain anchored her to the boat, to Finn's hand, to the fact she was in the water, shivering, the fact she couldn't swim, and the fact that, without her, Tucker would be lost in the dream world. Her arm throbbed with pain as four puncture wounds bled through her shirt. The world was still unfocused, the sounds far away, but the water was real, and she knew she needed to get out.

Reaching up with the other hand, she grabbed Finn's arm as he tried to pull her into the boat. The incongruity of the water and her bed fought in her mind. The pull to let go and sink back into the blissful oblivion of her covers drained the remainder of her adrenaline, which had kept her going across the water, and she fought to keep her eyes open. She kicked with her feet, resisting the force pulling her downward. Isabella surged up toward the edge of the boat with her last strength, then the world faded once again. Sleep. Sleep needed to come.

It was nearly dawn when she woke up, back against the sand on the opposite bank, Kimi curled up on her chest, the warmth of the fox radiating through her, warming her blood. She turned her head to see Finn worrying the lines tying their canoe to a tree stump on the bank. A small campfire was cracking happily between them. Her throat was sore, and her body ached like she'd been lifting heavy objects all night. She remembered very little about their trip.

"You're still with us," Kimi said, stretching her limbs as she hopped off Isabella's chest, leaving a cold and empty space. "Good." Then she walked into the woods, coming back a short time later with a small rabbit. Which she dropped near the fire. Then trotted happily over to Finn.

Isabella lay there, unwilling to speak or move for the moment, awake to a world she didn't understand. Last night was a strange mix of images she tried to splice together, slowly piecing the events together. She fell, no, she was pushed into the water. The shadow. No, it wasn't the shadow that shoved her. Then Finn or Kimi. Kimi on her hind legs, the boat leaning too far starboard. Then the strange feeling of peaceful memories of her parents and her brother. And the pain. Isabella looked at her arm. A white cloth was wrapped around it, four red dots, two above and two below.

"You bit me," she said, looking at Kimi.

"You're awake," Finn's voice was filled with relief. "Weaver's charms, I thought you were a goner."

"She bit me," Isabella sat up quickly, and her head spun the world like a top. Putting a hand to her temple, she tried to concentrate on not passing out. "She pushed me in, then she bit me."

"Izzy, I don't think Kimi did it on purpose."

"Oh, I bit her on purpose," Kimi said, taking a break from her rabbit.

"Not helping," Finn glowered at her.

"You heard her," Isabella scowled. "The shadow was right. She's trying to keep me from helping my brother. She wants him to be consumed by the dream world." She grabbed a stick off the ground and threw it at Kimi, missing by a wide berth.

"No, Izzy," Finn tried to calm her down, "you don't understand. You were delir—"

"No, Finn," Kimi left the rabbit and strode over to face Isabella, "let her say what she really wants to say."

"You are a selfish, inconsiderate, rude creature. You want me to fail, my brother to be trapped here," tears burned in Isabella's eyes. "All I want to do is rescue him, but you keep trying to stop me, you keep stopping me. I know you'll deny everything, but I know the truth, the shadow told me on the ice. These things you say are monsters have been the only thing to help me."

At the last part, Finn's eyes sparked, and he visibly winced. Shaking his head and exhaling loudly, Finn got up and walked back over to the boat, readying it for his trip home.

"That's not what I mean, Finn," Isabella backpedaled, but her heart wasn't in it, "I wasn't talking about you."

"See who she is now, Finnegan," Kimi turned to him, her voice cold and cruel, "the thanks we get for saving her life."

"That's not fair, and you know it," Isabella started.

"No," Kimi said, snarling at her. "You had your say, now I get mine. You think I'm selfish, I'm inconsiderate. Look in a mirror. I tried to warn you about the trap you were in. You went anyway, who found you the exit before it was too late. I knew what you thought was your brother was simply a shade, but you went after him, deeper in the trap. And yes, I bit you. I tasted your blood, sour as it is, but think about why, and if you can't figure it out, if you don't know what a friend looks like, then you— Then you are no Weaver, and you never will be. Let the shadows take you for all I care," Kimi's voice was hoarse at the end, choked off at parts, but the last part came through clear. "The shadows take you."

With that, she spurred the sand and took off into the underbrush like a streak of lightning, leaving Finn gaping at

Isabella and Isabella glaring at the woods cradling her arm close to her chest. For some reason she couldn't explain, she wanted to cry for an unexplainable loss aching deep inside.

⟶TWENTY⟵

Isabella watched as Kimi ran off into the undergrowth at the edge of the water. The profound loss she felt was overshadowed by the feeling of injustice. Kimi bit her, shoved her into the river, kept her from her brother, and ultimately wrote her off. The shadow's warning before all of this had begun was right. Isabella realized she couldn't trust Kimi, but even though she knew it, there was a part of her longing for that little red fox. Part of her felt she very much needed it.

"Of course," Finn said, exasperation clear in his voice, "the first weaver I meet is dysfunctional. Just my luck." He threw his pack into the boat and stood staring at her. His eyes completely unreadable.

"I'm not a weaver," Isabella's voice sounded weak and unsure even to her ears. "That *thing* is crazy."

"That *thing*, as you call it, is a companion," Finn shook his head. "They're never wrong about weavers."

"I'm not a—"

"No argument here," Finn went back to rearranging things in the canoe for his trip back across the now placid water. "You are definitely not a weaver, and if you don't fix things with Kimi, you probably never will be, just a walker or worse." It was evident by the drop in his voice Isabella wasn't supposed to hear the next part, "Given your love of the shadows, worse seems likely."

"What's that supposed to mean?"

Finn looked like he was caught cheating on a test, "Heard that last part, eh?"

Isabella nodded; she didn't trust herself to talk as she fought the tightness in the back of her throat. She knew Finn was leaving, but his words made her feel genuinely alone, like he was giving up on her too. Having him go was one thing, but having him pull away was entirely different for some reason.

"I guess you need to hear it anyway," he looked around as if he were letting her in on some deep secret the trees might be offended by. The sun began to peek over the horizon behind him, and he stood silhouetted against the brightening river. "These visitors—Dels' and Ajay keep telling me there's a difference between weavers and wanderers but they seem the same to me. Anyway, these visitors aren't the only people who come and go around here."

"I'm not in the mood for another one of your stories Finn," Isabella turned her back to him and crossed her arms. She studied the edge of the woods and the undergrowth for movement. Finn's hand grabbed her arm and gently turned her around.

"Seriously," he motioned to a rock on the edge of the water, "sit down. You need to hear this."

Isabella rolled her eyes and, without uncrossing her arms, sat hard on the rock. She uncrossed her arms for a moment to motion Finn should speak, then recrossed them and scowled at him. If he was abandoning her alone on the riverbank, she wasn't going to make anything easy for him.

"Alright," he took a seat facing her on the stern of the canoe; it rocked momentarily before he deftly balanced it, "here's the hard truth, not one of my stories, trust me." He watched her unchanged demeanor for a moment before continuing. "Besides the denizens, hunters like me, caretakers, and shadows, there are also people who seem to come and go from the world. The weavers and wanderers are among them. Most people say that visitors are like wanderers, but they can't seem to interact with us well as if they're only partly here. But there's a fourth type, you've heard me mention them, that's the stalkers. I do my best to stay away from them. Shadows are easy to handle, they almost seem to appreciate being taken out, if that makes any sense, but stalkers are dangerous. They're just as powerful as weavers, and if you've ever seen a weaver in action, you'd know that's some scary mojo. Ajay's told me about what he's seen, and he doesn't play. But while weavers try to help, stalkers only want to harm.

"I've only heard stories, but it's enough for me to know I want nothing to do with them. They bring people to the shadows, trap them in their illusions, almost seem to worship them. There are some denizens, some hunters even, who work with them— bad news if you ask me."

"Stories again," Isabella moved to get up.

"Right, but from a good source," Finn forestalled her. "I've never seen them, but Ajay was in with one hunter group before he found out they worked closely with a stalker. Way he tells it chills the blood."

Isabella considered the large Hindi man who she'd met coming into Finn's camp. She'd liked him immediately, plus Finn seemed to trust him completely, and for all of his faults, Finn seemed to be someone who surrounded himself with good people. Isabella flinched inwardly at the thought and the questions coming with this realization. Was she a good person, deserving of Finn's, or anyone else's, help and friendship? From her brief time at the camp, Finn and his friends were fiercely loyal to each other. Isabella thought about why she was even here, to save her brother from a place she'd sent him to, to fix the problem she caused. Dealing with your own mistakes isn't the same thing as loyalty.

"Way Ajay tells it," Finn continued when Isabella settled back onto the rock, "stalkers come from people who were supposed to be weavers, but they were corrupted somehow. Typically they have some deep-seated guilt over a mistake or having lost someone. They didn't start out bad, he says. It just happens. But they all have one thing in common," Finn looked at the undergrowth as he finished. "Their companions are gone. Dead or just separated, but it's like a part of them is missing, an important part if you ask me."

"Are you saying I'm corrupt?"

"No," he put his hands up in defense, "I'm not, not yet at any rate," he paused and took a deep breath. "I'm saying companions are important, and if you don't learn to accept Kimi for what and who she is, you could *become* corrupt," he flashed a toothy grin, but it wasn't mirrored in his eyes this time, "or at least that's what Ajay would say."

Isabella watched him, and for a little while, he met her gaze, but then he looked to the water and to his feet. She could almost see the war going on within him, and it gave her confidence. He had not given up on her, he was considering staying to help her going forward, and she was tempted for a breath to let him. Still, other people were relying on him, Ajay and the over-excited Delson who'd accosted him when they'd first gotten to camp. She thought if she asked him to stay and help her, he would, but at what cost? These were questions she didn't have an answer to, questions she didn't want to answer.

"Sun'll be up soon," she said, motioning behind him.

Finn looked over his shoulder at the brightening horizon behind him. The water was now calm and placid. She could make out the thin boat keeper searching the bank for something and thought of the knife in her pocket. She pulled it out and examined it for the first time. She'd managed to find the sheath for the knife after Kimi had shown herself, but now, seeing the man searching, she felt bad for taking it. The sheath was simple brown leather, and the handle was unfinished wood, made smooth by use, but the blade was thin and sharp, the tip slightly curved up. It was clear it had been loved. Finn noticed her looking at it and, glancing across the river, saw the man looking for it.

"Keep it," he said, "I'll explain."

"Are you sure?"

"Given how bad you are at the bow and how you tried to hold the arrow," Finn's smile was more genuine this time, "I'd say it's safer. Besides, you need something to protect yourself, and we lost some of the supplies when you fell into the water," he shrugged, "including your bow."

"You mean when Kimi pushed me into the water," she scowled.

"No, I mean when you fell in." Finn squinted at her, "Do you really believe Kimi pushed you?"

"Well," Isabella was beginning to feel the heat creep up her cheeks, "she did, didn't she?"

"No," he laughed humorlessly. "You were already overbalanced, Kimi got startled and bumped into you, but as she was recovering, your paddle smacked her back into the side, which was funny when you think about it. You fell in Izzy, almost swamped the whole canoe in the process."

"But she bit me."

"To break the hold the shadow had on you. She didn't bite you, she bit the shadow, but her teeth went right through into your skin." Finn's eyes widened in concern, "You honestly believed she– Oh Izzy," he looked pained, "you have this all wrong."

Isabella listened as Finn gave her a play-by-play of what happened when they were crossing the water. Kimi's worry when

Isabella had fallen in, how Finn physically retrained the little creature to stop her jumping in herself. He explained when they pulled her up, they'd almost lost her to a shadow who'd wrapped itself around her almost completely. How Kimi broke from under Finn's arm and tore into the shadow, ripping it free from Isabella and being thrown hard against the side of the canoe as it flailed. Kimi had woken only shortly before Isabella but had worried over her continually until she had woken herself.

"She's a proud creature," Finn concluded. "Loyal and courageous, but stubborn too. You need to find her Izzy," Finn looked between the water and the undergrowth, conflict written on his forehead. "Clear the air between the two of you, and I have a feeling you will be unstoppable. You're formidable enough on your own, but together–" he exhaled sharply and left the rest of his sentence unsaid.

Closing her eyes, Isabella took a deep breath; if what Finn told her was right, she owed Kimi an apology. If Kimi could help her save her brother, she had no choice but to apologize, whether or not Finn was telling her the truth. Isabella studied her feet, again she was tempted to ask Finn to come with her, but she knew it was not the right thing to do. He was expected back, and if, as Wren said, this world was not merely a figment of her subconscious, he was needed for something bigger than her or her brother.

"You're going to be late," she said after a long silence.

"Do you need–" Finn began.

Isabella stood up and held out her hand to stop him from asking the question she didn't know if she could say no to. "You're needed with the hunters, Ajay and Delson, Wren, they all need you. I've got this." She tried to make her voice sound confident, although she didn't feel it.

She noticed the look of relief on Finn's face. He would have stuck by her despite his promises. He hadn't been ready to abandon her like she'd feared, and if she'd been wrong about that, she could be wrong about Kimi. Isabella felt something in her swell at the thought, and she smiled at Finn's relief.

"You're sure?"

"No," she was honest, "but it's the right thing, and you know it." Looking at the underbrush resting silently on the bank in the early morning light, "Besides, I think this is something I need to do on my own."

"Good luck Isabella, future weaver," Finn said, standing up and extending his hand.

"Good luck to you, Finnegan, hunter of shadows," Isabella took his hand and pulled him into a hug, which he readily returned. They parted, and Isabella thought she saw the rising sun sparkle in Finn's eyes. She held his hand a moment longer and added, "My friend."

He smiled and, without preamble, headed for the canoe and pushed off. Isabella watched as he began to paddle across the peaceful river, last night's current all but nonexistent. She was about to turn and leave when he turned the canoe upriver and called back to her, "Tell Kimi I said bye." Before she could answer, he pivoted the canoe and quietly paddled back across the river.

Isabella smiled at his certainty she would get a chance to, a surety she wanted to share. "Sure thing," she whispered to the river, then she turned her back to the sun and began searching for a path into the still dark forest.

❧ TWENTY-ONE ❧

T he path she found started out easy, but as she pushed her way through the low hanging branches, Isabella was beginning to think this was more of an animal path than something she would be able to continue down much further. The sunrise at her back hadn't achieved much in the dense forest. Her shadow was longer, but so were other shadows, giving the surrounding trees an ominous feel. For a while now, Isabella had the feeling she was being watched but was sure it was just Kimi keeping her distance as usual. Realizing she wasn't actually alone in the forest gave her a sense of peace. She had misjudged Finn's initial reaction; apparently, she had misjudged Kimi's as well.

A muffled cry off the side of the path caught her attention, and she froze. This was not the call of a fox, there was something very human about the cry, and there was also something terrified about it. Isabella stood in the middle of the animal path and looked back and forth as far as she could see. There was no-one around. She thought about calling out for Kimi but didn't want to alert whoever was crying out and, maybe more importantly, whoever was causing the person to cry out. Instead, she crouched down and turned to her right. The sun filtered through the canopy, and she was occasionally blinded by a ray piercing the gloom of the forest.

Again, the muffled cry came, but it was louder this time, closer. Isabella pushed through the dense undergrowth next to the path and burst into a large open forest floor. The sun barely reached this deep into the forest, so there was very little light for the brambly plants to grow, unlike the outer edge and along the path. Isabella could see a darker shadow floating back and forth about a hundred yards ahead of her in the perennial dusk blanketing the forest floor. The flitting shadow would stop occasionally and roar at one bush or another. It seemed to be searching for something or someone, and it was not happy. Isabella didn't want to confront the agitated shadow and was about to sneak back to the path she'd been following, heading toward her brother, when she heard the voice crying out again. This time, the shadow seems to zero in on the whimpering cry and floated nearer a bush to the left of the clearing it occupied.

The voice sounded young, older than her brother, but still young. It wasn't the words the voice called, but it was the tone which made her act, a sad and helpless tone, calling out for everything the child had known and had loved. Isabella acted before she thought everything through.

"Hey," she called out to the shadow, "hey there. Any clue how to get to the mall from here?" It sounded like a strange thing to yell in the middle of the woods, but she couldn't think of anything else. Strange or not, it worked.

The shadow turned toward her. Its dark, misty form swirled and seemed to swell as the colorless eyes fell on her. Spinning away from the bush where it had cornered the child, who Isabella could see shaking and watching the shadow with wide eyes, the shadow let out a shrill shriek filled with pain and sadness. The child in the bushes flinched as the sound washed over him. Isabella could feel the hairs on her arms raise as if by static electricity, and goosebumps spread across her skin. The shadow stood to its full height, dwarfing the low bushes surrounding it, and rushed at Isabella.

"Stop," she called out, her voice seeming to reverberate around the forest for a moment before the shadow came to a slowing stop before her.

"Why have you interfered with my hunt?" the shadow's voice was almost as insubstantial as the creature itself. It reverberated, but unlike Isabella's voice, which folded out to fill the trees, the shadow's voice echoed inward, off of itself, giving it a hollow sound that sent involuntary shivers down Isabella's spine.

"I have met one of you before," she tried to keep her tone conversational.

"And survived," the words were somewhere between a statement and a question.

Isabella continued as if it hadn't spoken; she tried desperately to figure out what to say to get this thing to stop harassing the kid, or at least keep it talking long enough for the kid to escape. With the shadow having cornered the poor kid, Isabella thought Finn and Kimi might be right about the shadows after all, but she still wasn't positive the shadows were evil. She went with the only thing she could think of, hoping it distracted the shadow long enough for the kid to get away. "He showed me where my brother was. I was hoping you would do the same."

The shadow produced a sound that could have been intended as a laugh, but to Isabella's ears, it sounded more like nails drawn down a chalkboard. "I will help you find your brother."

"Why thank you," Isabella smiled, she wanted to believe the shadow knew where her brother was, and although part of her was warning against it, she let herself trust the thing in front of her. She'd have to tell Finn all about this shadow helping the next time she saw him. Maybe she could work a truce out between the groups.

"You are mistaken, child," the menace and cruelty flowing from the shadow was impossible to miss, "I will help you find your brother, but then I will make you watch as I break him and make him one of us. You will have no choice but to be one of ours then."

"One of yours?" Isabella thought back to Finn's explanation of the Stalkers and shuddered.

"Your ignorance is my friend," the shadow moved closer to her, its glossy claws extending, clicking together in the dappled shadows of the trees. "Your anger and defiance will serve me nicely." Isabella couldn't stop looking at the claws weaving together in a rhythmic clicking. She couldn't look away, felt drawn to the sound. Something was comforting about the noise. It was like a heartbeat or a clock ticking away on a cold winter's night.

"We will find my brother together," she said. "He needs your help."

"And I will help him," the greed in the shadow's voice didn't register in Isabella's ears. "He will have a long life here with us, and you will forever be there to watch over him."

Isabella liked the friendliness in the shadow's voice. His claws were less menacing, more open, accepting. Its form seemed to widen more, the edges of the shadow swirling around her feet and hands. What it was saying made sense, felt good. Her brother would be safe here with the shadow, and she finally understood. Kimi, Finn, Wren, they had it all wrong. The shadows were here to save people, rescue them. She'd done the boy a disservice when she called the shadow away from him; she wouldn't do the same to her brother.

As these thoughts drifted through her head, Isabella was faintly aware they felt wrong, foreign somehow. Part of her tried to remember what made her call the shadow from the boy in the bushes, but she couldn't place the feeling. A vague sadness washed over her at the thought of her mother and father, who seemed so far away. She thought of Finn and Kimi's misguided crusade against these benevolent shadows, and a pang of guilt pulsed through her.

She became vaguely aware of movement beside her, a blur of color in a world of browns and grays. Something slammed into the side of her, knocking her from her feet, and Isabella landed hard on the ground, bruising her left shoulder on an exposed root. The sound of a rushing river overwhelmed her ears as images flash before her of her brother wandering on a riverbank, Finn dangling from a fallen tree reaching his arms out, Kimi sitting proudly on a colorful picnic table. She looked up from the cold, damp ground and a massive shadow loomed over her, its claws extending toward a small red fox who leaped deftly back, snarling at the shadow.

Isabella instantly became aware of the menace and pain flowing off the shadow like a waterfall and scurried backward, her back pushed against the trunk of a tree, as the shadow turned its claws toward her. A cry of pain and sadness emanated from the creature, and it lunged toward Isabella, who was frozen in horror, but before the claws even reached her, Kimi dove through the shadow, teeth and claws bared in anger, and it dissipated in swirls of dark fog. Kimi landed and skid to a stop in front of Isabella, who panted to get her breathing under control.

"Kimi," she manages through gasps as the adrenaline drained from her system.

"I have not forgiven you," she says before Isabella can get any more words out. "Don't mistake my kindness for anything it is not. You have shown time and again, you do not trust me, and I will not argue the point with you. I saved you this time because you did the right thing in saving the boy."

"Did he make it out?" Isabella's words bust through the shock, "Is he safe?"

"He did," Kimi stood up and looked back toward the bush where the boy had been hiding.

"Thank you for following me despite my—"

Kimi turned her eyes back to Isabella and narrowed them, "I have not followed you. When I said the shadows could have you, I meant it."

"But then how— you're here now, you helped me."

"I am looking for Finn and Wren," her tone was matter-of-fact, "since you will not accept your part in this world, I will do it for you. I will join them to defeat the Shadow Congress. I heard the boy, just like you, and came to help him. You had already done so, and I could not let you pay the price for helping someone who could not help themselves."

"I'm sorry I didn't trust you," Isabella rested her elbows on her knees and leaned her head back against the tree, closing her eyes as her breathing finally came back to normal.

"The apology is nice to hear, but it is too late, Isabella," Kimi's voice was stern, determined. "I have made too many efforts to connect with you, and you have not been willing. You have shown me nothing but disgust for the kindnesses I have done you, and in time, this one will be no different. You will twist my actions to fit your narrative, you will make yourself the victim of my plans, and your path will forever be dark. Maybe if we had met years from now, things would be different, but you are here now, and things are what they are."

Isabella could feel tears burning behind her still closed eyes. She couldn't bring herself to open them and look at Kimi. She knew now, she'd been unfairly judging the small red fox, but now it seemed like she was too late to change anything.

"I am truly sorry for you, Isabella Shaw," and Kimi did sound sad, "but this is goodbye." There were several seconds of silence after she finished talking, and Isabella, scarcely able to breathe, wished she would change her mind. A rustling in the underbrush told Isabella she was now genuinely alone under this forbidding canopy. The warmth she had felt when she thought Kimi had been following her had turned to a hollow ache, and Isabella drew her knees closer to her chest and considered the ever-encroaching darkness of the forest.

TWENTY-TWO

The path seemed more challenging, the roots more frequent, as Isabella moved deeper into the thickening forest, searching for her brother. When she stumbled for the fourth time, yelping as she scraped her knee on another exposed rock, she knelt and dug her fingers into the dirt, trying to take out her frustration on something. Never had someone so clearly give up on her, so thoroughly written her out of the equation, then Kimi. Sure, she'd upset her mother, disappointed her teachers, made her brother cry, but they always came back. They had to. Kimi, on the other hand, Kimi didn't, and Isabella felt the loss of her more keenly than she'd felt anything.

"Stop moping," she said, pushing herself out of the dirt. "You brought this on yourself, now fix it." She looked down the path, it had begun to incline about an hour after the incident with the shadow, and it hadn't leveled out since.

The sun had risen higher in the sky, and the heat had followed. Sweat dripped down between her shoulder blades and beaded on her forehead. She'd rolled up her sleeves before emptying half of the waters-skin Finn had given her, but she refused to drink anymore because her brother had been out as long as she had. He would need the water more than she did, and she was going to make sure there was enough for him.

She trudged through the mangled path for another hour, her hope dwindling with each step. She was so sure when she'd set out this was the correct path, but each passing hour made the surety seem less substantial and more like a shot in the dark. Ahead, the way separated into two paths, one heading north and the other keeping west. She stood at the intersection and tried to peer down each as far as she could, but she couldn't see a difference. Standing there at the crossroads, Isabella felt the cold hand of panic begin to seize her heart.

There was no evidence which path would work; instead, she closed her eyes and tried to listen like she had when she'd heard the boy. The sound was faint at first, but distinct, humming. It wasn't just humming; she knew the song. It was one her mother had sung to both her and her brother for years.

For a moment, the voice of her mother's signing overshadowed the humming she heard, *Too ra loo ra loo ral.* Isabella's breath caught in her throat, and she pushed her mother's voice from her head and listened for the humming again. This time it was clear, but she couldn't tell yet which path the sound was coming from. Closing her eyes, she tried to imagine what it looked like down each direction, but the humming was still there, receding, getting harder to hear with each passing moment. She felt like the sound was coming from the north, but she wasn't sure. She knew the sound would fade from hearing all too soon, so she had to make a choice. As she set her foot on the north path, Isabella knew it was the right one. She could feel her brother here, closer than she'd been this whole time.

"Tucker," she whispered, "I'm coming." Clods of dirt flew behind her as she raced down the path, heedless of roots and rocks strewn throughout the ground. The path curved around a large ash tree sprouting from the middle of the trail, towering above the canopy. As she reached the warm protectiveness of the dappled sun beneath the expansive tree, she leaned against the silvery bark to catch her breath. Here she felt safe, this felt like an island in the middle of a stormy sea, and she was tempted to stay there, but the humming was fading again, and she knew her brother was in danger in these woods. She would not leave him to the shadows or abandon him in this gloomy forest.

Reluctantly she pushed away from the tree and began down the path again. At its zenith, the sun shone golden through the leaf-filled branches spreading out impossibly far in all directions. Isabella sighed and quickened her pace; Tucker was close—she could feel it.

"Tucker," she called out, not caring what other dangers she might call her way. The humming stopped, and Isabella held her breath, waiting for a response. The wind rustled the leaves on the branches overhead, and the silence stretched out ahead of her. Fearing the worst, she ran again down the silent path.

"Iee-iee?" A small voice came from the path ahead.

"Tucker, buddy," she called through burning lungs, "I'm here."

At the sight of him, sitting by the edge of the path, eating some strange fruit, Isabella thought her heart might explode. The juice from the fruit was covering his hands and ran down his chin. The dirt of the forest clung in the sticky rivets across his face. He smiled when he saw her and dropped his snack on the ground to the side of the path. With the swiftness of the very young, he ran over to her and caught hold of her legs. "Sister," he cried into her knees, "worried sister. Spookies. Spookies chase me."

"I know, buddy," she crouched down and kissed the dirt on his face. "I'm so sorry it took me so long to get here."

"It okay," he smiled. "Go home now." A big smile glowed on his face, and he began to pull her down the path in the direction they were headed.

Looking ahead, Isabella saw the change in the light before she noticed the reason. About fifty yards ahead of them, the light in the forest became brighter, the trees thinned out, but everything growing there had a pale, sickly color. Isabella recognized it immediately as the area the shadow had shown her on the frozen lake. Tucker was pulling her toward it with renewed energy as they got closer. She could feel a coldness closing around them as if the heat of the afternoon couldn't penetrate to the forest floor.

"Tucker," Isabella planted her feet, "not that way, buddy."

He pulled on her arm, "Sister, go home now." He smiled at her and pulled, grunting showily with the effort.

"No," she said, pulling her hand back, "danger there."

"Not danger," he said and smiled, "home." Tucker turned and ran down the path.

"Tucker," Isabella called after him, her feet reluctant to move ahead. "Stop, buddy." Her voice seemed once again to reverberate in the trees. Tucker stopped and slowly made his way back to Isabella, reluctantly giving up the ground he'd made in his mad dash home.

"Home sister," he insisted, "go home now."

"Not that way," she turned him around to head back the way they came, but noises down the path stopped her. She was almost sure of what it was even before her blood ran cold. "Shadows."

"Spookies," Tucker said, hiding behind her leg, "Bad guys."

"I know buddy," Isabella searched for someplace to hide, her eyes skirting the underbrush. "Let's play hide and seek?"

"Okay," Isabella knew her brother could never say no to a game of hide-and-seek.

"I'm it, so I'll count," Isabella watched as the shadows moved through the trees all around her. "Hide in there until they're gone. Big sister's got this."

Tucker let go of her leg and rushed to the bramble on the side of the path. It rustled a little as he situated himself, then was silent. Tucker loved hide and seek, and was generally good at it, so she knew he'd be quiet in there. With Tucker safely out of the way, the chill in the air became more noticeable, and Isabella shrugged on her jacket she'd been carrying since the heat had picked up again. She searched her pockets for something she could use to defend herself. Her hands first found the dream catcher the old woman had given her, still tucked into her jacket pocket. The only other thing she felt was the forgotten fishing knife. As the shadows broke the cover of the trees, Isabella drew the knife and held it blade down like she'd seen in the movies her father liked to watch.

As the first shadow approached, the feelings of anger and pain cascaded from it in rivers of sorrow. Isabella fought to overcome the onslaught of emotions and took a swing at the advancing shadow. Seeing her swipe coming, the shadow unformed and reformed as her hand went through, its insubstantial body eddying in the wake of her hand.

The shadow, completely unharmed, tilted its head to the sky and shrieked. The sound coming from the creature was painful to hear and grated on her already turbulent emotions. Isabella recovered quickly, but the shadow had moved closer and was pulling its hand back to strike. Isabelle rolled out of the way, grabbing swathes of dirt to throw in the thing's face. Rolling onto her back, Isabella let the dirt fly. The shadow simply folded around it, reforming as the dirt sprinkled to the ground harmlessly behind it. Kimi and Finn had made this look and sound easy, but she'd missed gloriously.

Another shriek emanated from the shadow's upturned face. A rustle in the undergrowth made Isabella's heart soar, Kimi had returned to help her again in a time of need, but Kimi didn't spring from the brush where it crashed and waved. Instead, her brother rose on unsteady legs and ran down the path away from the shadows toward the forest's desolated area.

"Tucker, wait," Isabella cried out from the ground. She couldn't let him get to the deadened forest area. The shadow's warning echoed in her ears: *His time is short. Once he crosses from the greenery to the dark heart of the woods, he will be trapped in the dreamworld forever.* Heedless of the shadows emerging from all around, Isabella pushed herself off the dirt once more and ran full tilt toward her little brother. "Tucker, stop."

He either didn't hear her or didn't want to stop because, despite her panicked calls, Tucker ran straight past the line dividing the rich green of the forest from the cold gray of the deadened area. Isabella skidded to a stop at the edge, calling out to her brother, tears falling unchecked down her face, "Tucker." Calling over and over again.

She felt the shadows approached, but for the moment she shared Kimi's opinion, the shadows could take her. She'd failed at her duty. Her brother, her innocent bright-eyed brother, would now be trapped in the dream world forever, and it was all her fault. She couldn't keep him safe, and now, he was trapped here. She failed him.

One of the shadows broke off from the others and came before her. The unformed darkness flowed across the forest floor until it floated just a few feet in front of her. Fear and despair ebbed from it in waves, but Isabella stood her ground. The shadow did not advance; instead, it floated where it was, intermittently blocking the dappled light from the descended sun.

"You again," despite there being no makings, no features to distinguish this shadow from the one Kimi had killed not long before, Isabella knew this was the one who had visited her on the ice, had shown her where her brother was. This was the shadow that began everything, and for one moment, she thought about striking it with the fishing knife just for trying to talk to her again.

"There is nothing you can do for your brother," his hollow voice didn't echo on itself; instead, it hung in the air like a mist.

"You've lied to me before," Isabella remembered his warnings against Kimi and her fist curled around the knife in her pocket. "I don't believe you."

"You don't have to believe me for it to be true." His answer fell like fog from his ever-shifting face.

"It doesn't matter," Isabella looked at the divide between the green forest in which she stood and the gray landscape her brother fled into, "I need to go after him."

"Go if you wish," the shadow moved aside to let Isabella past, "but know once you step over, your world will be lost to you. You will never wake again in your bed to your mother's songs. You may gain your brother, but you will lose everything else."

Isabella stood on the path between the silent shadows and desolation her brother rushed into, watched the gray flakes float in the air before her. Images of her parents and friends at school flashed before her eyes. Her mother's lilting songs, her father's deep laugh, the joy of spending time with her friends. All swirled through her mind with her brother's laughter and tears—his hugs and screams. Isabella watched the flecks of gray billow and dance eerily in the sunlight shining coldly before her.

TWENTY-THREE

The world before her stood as a stark reversal from the luscious forest she'd been traveling through. The trees stood empty, the bark a flaking gray, where the underbrush was thick on the paths she'd taken to get here, the way ahead of her laid bare, gray ash framed the worn dirt. The air, here clear and crisp, ahead of her various motes of gray ash floating as if there was a fire burning deeper in. The shadow's warning still echoed in her ears while she watched her brother's back fading into the laden air.

"Tucker," she called to him, but he didn't turn.

"He won't hear you calling him from here," the shadow's voice was hollow as if all emotion had been drained away, and for the first time, Isabella wondered how the shadows became shadows. Where the nightmares populating this world, the unformed fears of dreamers, or was there something more sinister in the people's dreams?

"Then I have no choice, do I?"

"You have the choice to leave," there was a strange tenor in the shadow's voice, matching in its form; a shiver seemed to go through it. "We will not stop you if you head to the ash tree now. From there, you can leave. You do not have the same promise if you go forward."

"But my brother–"

"Is already lost to you."

A pain sharper than any cut wrenched through her at those words, and her shouldered sagged. She had failed him, failed her parents, and now she would have to go home and watch her family search in vain, crushed under the weight of the truth. The truth was if she was stronger, if she was smarter, more patient, braver– if she were like Finn or Wren, like Kimi, then her brother would be safe at home in his crib. She turned and looked back down the path she'd come from; the shadows who chased her brother had moved aside to let her pass. Their emotions a roil of greed, desperation, pain, and hunger unchanged despite their apparent deference to the one who spoke with her. Under everything was fear; there was no loyalty, no joy in their actions. They were fed by and lived in fear. It was something she could understand.

"You have made your choice then," the hollow shadow intoned behind her.

"I have," Isabella turned back to it and smiled sadly, she understood the difference now, between the Weavers and the

Stalkers, between the denizens and the shadows, and it was such a small thing, but that little thing was everything. "Thank you." She bowed her head to the shadow standing at the edge of desolation.

The shadow straightened up and seemed to pulse with emotion once again; fear and despair, clear and sour, coursed from the insubstantial creature as it moved to join the others who seemed to pull away from it. For a moment, Isabella pitied the shadows. Their life was ruled by inaction and fear. They looked for those like them, those who were paralyzed by indecision because things might not go as they planned. They thrived on others' failure because failure bred fear, and fear still more until effort became impossible.

They pegged her right; she was just like them. She felt the fear and disappointment of failure, the bitterness that comes from watching others succeed while she barely kept her head above water. The anger at relying on others to save her time after time, the blame she placed on them and herself because of her inaction. She let these emotions flow through her and felt their power and felt their draw because they were easy choices. She closed her eyes and took a deep breath in, held it for a moment to calm her flailing heart, and exhaled slowly and deliberately.

With a smile curling her lips, she realized the shadow had been right, and with the realization, she flashed her sweetest smile at the line of shadows, skipped on her left foot, and pivoted into the desolation. Isabella realized she'd made her decision the moment Tucker had crossed out of the vibrant green forest into the desolate gray heart, as the shadow had called it. She wasn't sure she knew the whole story about crossing the line, but she knew the shadow had lied to her before, had lied about Kimi, and Isabella paid the price for believing it. That was not a price she would pay again.

Whether the shrieks from behind her meant the shadows were celebrating a victory or she thwarted their plans was far less critical than the fact that they were getting closer. She'd been given safe passage back to the ash tree, but forward into the ashy air, safety was not promised. She kicked up plumes of ash as she sped down the path toward Tucker's bounding back. She caught up with him as he tried to struggle over a fallen log blocking the way. She caught him in her arms and, scooping him up, slid over the log, landing hard on the other side. She felt her ankle twist and pain shoot up her left leg. The sound of the shadows was almost on top of them, and with nowhere to hide, Isabella used her body to cover her brother, intending to protect him from the shadow's claws.

"Iee iee," he said, through hitching sobs, "spookies chasing me."

"I know, buddy," she kissed the back of his head, her tears dampening his golden hair graying in the ash, "I got you." But the promise sounded hollow even to her ears. She could feel the emotions from the shadows pressing down on her, and she hugged her brother tighter. "I love you, buddy."

The sunlight cut diagonally across her bedroom, and shifting beneath her comforter, Isabella groaned, feeling overwhelmed and tired. Her pillow was wet with sweat, and her hair was in her face. She clutched at the edge of her blankets and whimpered against the rising sun. A brief sob wracked her prone shape, and then her eyes flew open to the approaching dawn. She lay in her bed, a place she had never expected to see again after crossing the threshold in the forest, but one she was happy to be in.

If she was here, her brain retraced her paces, trying desperately to catch up to reality. She didn't know if what she was remembering happened or if it was all a dream. In the curtained room, the light from the window angled over to the bars of her brother's crib. Wedged there, between the bars, Leo hung half dangling in mid-air, and Isabella's heart soared. Where her mother made his bed before she'd gone to sleep, the covers were now thrown back, bunched by the crib's foot.

Throwing her covers back, Isabella raced to the door of her room, pausing only long enough to pull the lonely lion from his prison in the bars, and carefully opened the door. She edged out in the hallway, afraid if she made noise, whatever hope bloomed in her heart would shatter and crumble away. Sounds rose from downstairs, a spoon in a bowl, a metal skillet being placed on the burners, and voices. She walked to the top of the stairs and listened down at the conversations below.

"Should we wake her up for pancakes?" Her mother's lilting musical voice was calm, peaceful in a way she hadn't heard since Tucker disappeared.

"Let's not," her father, "she's been through a lot in the past few days."

"I just wish–" her mother trailed off or was too quiet to hear more. Isabella's heart sank. There was not a joy in that last statement. She had been through a lot, but she was sure it wasn't what they were talking about.

"Pancakes," the exuberance in the voice was both unmistakable and enchanting to Isabella. She slipped down the first few stairs in her excitement at hearing her brother's voice. The noise brought the sound of chairs moving in the kitchen.

"Izzy," her mother called up, "are you alright."

"I'm fine," she said, rounding the corner into the kitchen and grabbing her brother, who squealed in delight. "You're here," she had tears in her eyes, which she didn't bother trying to hide. "I missed you, buddy." She set him down in his chair and ruffled his hair.

"Again, again," he called, standing up and jumping on his chair. Isabella wrapped her arms around him and breathed in the scent of his hair.

"Well, you're sure in a good mood," her mother walked over to hug her. Isabella set her brother down and squeezed her mother tightly, laughing with relief. "Didn't hurt yourself on the stairs?"

"My ankle hurts a little," Isabella said, aware for the first time her ankle did indeed hurt, "but it's fine. I'm fine. I'm home."

"Where else would you be, Izzy-bell?" The batter her father poured on the skillet sizzled, and the smell of cinnamon pancakes filled the room. "Hungry? I made pancakes, a sort of welcome home."

"Welcome home?"

"You know," he turned around and smiled at her, "from my business trip." He looked at her mother and back to Isabella, "Seriously, Izzy, are you alright?"

Isabella went to the cabinet and took out four glasses, set them on the table, and went to get the milk. "I'm fine dad," she was indeed home. After breakfast, Tucker and their mother went into the living room to play with his trains, and Isabella helped her father with the dishes.

"I had the strangest dream last night," Isabella said, handing her father another dirty plate, careful to avoid getting syrup on her.

"What was that?"

"Tucker disappeared in the middle of the night, and I went into this strange dream world to chase him down," she felt foolish describing it to him, but something about the tenseness in his shoulders worried her. "You told me before you wove dreams. What did you mean?"

"That," he looked at her and smirked, "was to get you to go back to sleep. You know I do like to sleep at night sometimes."

"Well, in my dream, I wove Tucker this dream and sent him into the dream world. I tried to follow him to bring him home."

"You always were a creative one, Izzy," he said, putting the last dish into the drying rack. "Why don't you head upstairs and get yourself changed. We can head out to get the stuff for your project, start the day off right."

"Sure thing," she walked out of the kitchen, stifling a laugh about her crazy dream, and paused for a moment at the bottom of the stairs to watch her mother and brother playing on the floor with his little wooden tracks. He still wore the same footed pajamas he had on in her dream, but they didn't seem as bright now.

Isabella took the stairs two at a time and, going to her room, flicked open her laptop to check the assignment's requirements while she got changed. Picking out jeans and a white blouse, Isabella sat down at the computer. The screen saver, flicking through nature pictures, showed one she hadn't seen before, a red fox standing on a log in a burned-out forest. Isabella moved the mouse and typed her password. After jotting down the requirements, she quickly checked her email as she doodled on the pad next to her computer.

"You ready yet, Izzy?" her father called from downstairs.

Ripping off the page, Isabella looked around her room. Everything was as she'd left it. Whether it was a dream or she somehow transported herself into another world, she wasn't sure, but things were back to the way they should be. Her father was home, her brother was home. Looking at the sheet she'd written, Izabella realized she'd doodled over the words and couldn't make them out. "Hold on a moment," she called down to her father, "just getting something."

"Hurry up," he called up uncommonly agitated, "I want to get to the store before the crowds."

Isabella walked over to the computer and typed in her password, watching the asterisks fill the white rectangle. But as the image on her screen cleared, she scanned her desktop. The icons looked familiar, but the letters under them didn't make words. She thought about pulling up the assignment requirements. She remembered writing them down, but she didn't remember what they were. She didn't even remember reading them. She remembered checking her email, but she couldn't think of a single message she'd read. Looking at the paper again, she noticed at the bottom was the rough sketch of a fox, drawn crudely, but she was never much of an artist. Her eyes darted to her bed and her brother's crib as the reality sunk in.

Downstairs she could hear her mother's voice muted by the door and her brother's giggling as train noises. Isabella walked over to her bookshelf and pulled out a random book; flipping through it left her no doubts. When her mother's laughter filtered through the door again, but the musical lilt was gone. Isabella felt her heart drop once more into her stomach as her breath caught in the throat.

"No," she said as she closed the book, a picture of a red fox emblazoned the cover. She closed her eyes and took a deep breath before tossing the book on her bed. Isabella glared at the closed door, "Not this time."

TWENTY-FOUR

Izzy," her father's voice called up the stairs, "you ready yet?" His voice, his words, they sounded like him, and Isabella struggled to break the image. She wanted him to be there because it meant she didn't have to solve her own problems. He could take over for her, keep Tucker safe because she'd already failed, and even if it isn't real, she could convince herself it is—until she couldn't. That final realization is what shook her confidence. She would willingly let someone else, a shadow of her parents, take care of her brother, of her.

"Coming," she balked at calling it dad.

Hanging on the back of her door was a dreamcatcher. Something about it looked oddly familiar; two woven branches intertwined, bright purple and green leather webbed together into two separate smaller circles, open in the center and dotted with turquoise beads. Small crystals within each circle caught the light and threw prisms across the door. Three leather tassels, filled with beads, each ending in a feather, hung from the outside. She took the delicate-looking piece off the hook she didn't remember being on her door and, grabbing her jacket off the back of her chair, put it in her pocket. She searched the other pockets of her coat for the old fishing knife but came up empty. Her boots sat by the door, where she'd always left them, and for a moment, she entertained the thought she may be reading too much into things. Glancing at the bookshelf erased any doubt because all the symbols on the edges of her books, where the titles should be, were indecipherable.

Slipping into her boots, Isabella turned the handle and moved into the hall. The downstairs was quiet, so her brother and what was attempting to pass as her mother weren't around. The other one waited at the door to the kitchen, keys in hand.

"Ready to go, Izzy?" it asked her. "I figure we can—" Isabella didn't stop. She walked past it into the kitchen and looked around. "Hey, what's up?"

She walked past again, not acknowledging her father's shape, and went to the living room. Her brother's pajamas were on the floor in a corner, and the train set abandoned on the floor.

"Tucker?" A knot formed in the pit of her stomach. There was no answer, but the shape of her father moved into the room.

"Izzy," it said, using his voice, "what's wrong? You're not behaving like yourself."

"Where are they?" She stood in the center of the room, right hand on her hip, Tucker's pajamas dangling from her extended left hand. "What have you done?"

"Done?" a stern look came to its face. "Young lady, you should have some more respect for your father."

"I do," she narrowed her eyes at the thing in the room with her, "now, where are they? Where is he?"

"That's how it is?"

"That's how it is," she threw the pajamas on the floor, glaring at the thing before of her as fear and desperation began to flood the room. "You can stop hiding, your trap is sprung, and I've gotten out of it before. I will do it again."

"I don't doubt you can," the voice sounded hollower than her father's voice, and she was glad it changed. The change removed all doubt. "But it doesn't leave much hope for your brother if you do. Leave this house, and it will be gone."

He didn't clarify what it was, her escape, the house, her reality, whatever reality was at this point, and she didn't ask. "Where is he?"

The voice returned to a facsimile of her father's voice, "He and your mother went for a walk around the block."

"Drop the act," Isabella took two steps toward the image of her father, "you do not exist."

"That is where you are wrong, Busy-Izzy," the edges of her father's shape blurred. "I do exist." With those words, the form dissolved into a shadow looming over her, tendrils extending out, filling the room with desperation. She felt the fear tug at her resolve and rational thought. The shadow dominated the space between her and the exit. The only way out blocked by the wafting creature; it laughed. "I exist despite your best attempts, but you will not. I could end you right now," its claws clicked on the wall next to the door, rivets of decay descending from where it touched. Ash filled the air, and Isabella coughed, covering her nose with her sleeve. "I could choke you out, remove the air from this room, and I will still exist." It moved its hand from the wall, and the air cleared. "I could draw one finger across your chest, plunge my hand in, and I will exist. You will not. You live because I let you—because your fear is pleasant to me.

"Don't look so surprised. I can feel your fear, your doubt, your guilt. Those are what drive you. Those are what keep you going, and those are what I will use to destroy you—to end you. But your end will be all the sweeter because it will only come after you have been completely broken. You have brought me your first tribute, you have sacrificed your brother to me, and I will not forget the importance of such a gift. I will reward you, and you will survive this place," it motioned toward the room. "You will leave this place and return to your world, your little life, but you will long to be back here. Here where there is true power. You will come back, and together we will build a new world here at the center of the night when the witching hours last beyond the rising of a frozen sun. Just leave through the door," a blue door hung on the wall behind the couch, "and you will be home safe in your bed.

"Of course, it's too late for your brother, but we will keep him safe here. He will be cared for by your mother and me, ignorant of where he is, his sleep will be dreamless, and he will be forever a child. You can even visit him from time to time. Eventually, you will realize you belong here, you belong with him, with me, and together we will bring both worlds to heel."

His words pulled at her, her fear and guilt welled up inside her, doubt rushed in like a river threatening to carry her away with the current of his words. The shadow coalesced back into her father's form, still standing in the door, leaning on the frame, the lines of decay on the wall beside him.

"What do you say, Izzy-bell?" His stance said confidence, but his voice held sarcasm like a shield against self-doubt.

Isabella took a deep breath and let out a sigh, intentionally sagging her shoulders and dropping her eyes to the floor. She could see her father's face in the periphery of her vision, and the sneer etching itself there was so unlike him any illusions she had would have been shattered. Realizing the fear drowning her was not her own. She did not have to own the pain in the room, the raging river of shame, because this wasn't over. She squeezed her eyes closed and took another breath. As she did, she pictured Finn laughing with Delson in the camp, Wren standing with her hawk on her shoulder, and Kimi racing through the grass. Their belief in her, their faith she was better than she thought filled her, and she raised her eyes, smiling sadly back at the shadow of her father in the door. "Looks like I have no other choice then."

"Honestly," he said, smiling warmly, "you never did."

"You may be right there," she said and began to move toward the door where he stood. "I just need to know one thing before I go."

"Anything for my daughter," it said, the sarcasm dropping to a false warmth, a picture of the loving father she knew.

"How does it feel to be so wrong all the time?" With the question, she kicked Tucker's pajamas into its face and rushed through the door. Behind her, she could hear the shriek of the shadow, the full weight of fear and desperation flashed outward behind her, but it was too late. She reached the front room and, throwing chairs behind her, raced to the door. She threw the door open onto a bright morning in suburban America and crashed through, slamming it behind her. She heard a sucking sound as the door closed.

Standing on her street that was not her street, Isabella looked around the familiar buildings. The flowers bloomed, and people were out mowing their lawns. People she recognized but did not know waved to her as she sped down the sidewalk. Her brother was in this place somewhere, in the twisted streets of her home town, where the familiar was not safe, and reality was a dream. He was out here with their mother, who was not their mother, a shadow mother, and she would find them.

No birds sang, no sound of mowers lazily trod across already short lawns. Isabella wondered how many of these people were shadows, lurking in the open, waiting for the opportunity to strike her down. Not letting the uncertainty distract her, she kept her thoughts focused on Tucker; finding him was what mattered. The blue door leading to safety was gone, and she didn't know if there would be another, but that would have to be a problem for another time.

The ground beneath her feet rumbled faintly, and while her mind raced back to the cottage, her eyes shot to the horizon. Stretching out around her, as far as she could see, were a maze of houses and streets she knew, but in the distance, the air was beginning to churn with dust and darkening clouds. She knew what was coming this time, and while she was scared of failing her brother once again, she knew she needed to try. In a matter of time, the ground would literally fall out from under her, but when she looked at the clouds bulging all around, she smiled. Isabella realized the very force bent on her destruction would be what saved her, and with a cry of defiance and victory, she set off at a run toward where she knew her brother would go, to the very place he needed to be.

Every time they went for a walk, whenever Isabella had been forced to bring her brother someplace to get out of her parents' hair during the summer when the weather was nice, he would beg to go to the playground in the center of their neighborhood. Right now, she thought, looking at the billowing clouds surrounding her, the center was exactly where she needed him to be. With an excited cry, Isabella jumped up and spun, careful to land on her uninjured leg, and took off at a hobbling jog. This was not over, she thought as fear threatened to overtake her once more and the clouds on the horizon grew. This was not over by a long shot.

❧ TWENTY-FIVE ❧

The ground rumbled almost continuously now, but still faint. Given the distance she'd already run through the neighborhood, this seemed like a much bigger trap than the last one, and Isabella wondered how long they planned on keeping them here, playing with their emotions. The playground was up ahead, but it was quiet, eerily so. No sounds of creaking swings as they swayed with the slight breeze, no sounds of children playing, no laughter, or calling out the rules of their games. Instead, the playscape, which intimidated her enough as a kid, looked like an M.C. Escher sketch. The platforms looked twice as tall and half as wide as she remembered, while the slides looked so steep they would shoot a full-sized adult into the ground, forget about a kid. Ladders climbing onto the platforms were crooked and impossibly spindly, while the tunnels were so small she wasn't sure she would be able to get through them.

When she reached the gate of the play area, benches lining the edges, she saw her brother sitting on the edge of a giant sandbox, a yellow dump truck plowing through the sands. He looked small against the oversized playscape, and while he wheeled the truck back and forth over the sand, he looked up from time to time as if hoping someone would come to play with him. Isabella walked over; it seemed odd for him to be by himself, but the shadow mother wasn't their real mom, so who knew what she intended.

"Having fun?" Isabella asked, standing behind her brother as he hunched over the truck in the sand.

At first, he flinched at the sound of her voice, but then he relaxed and looked suspiciously behind him. For a moment, Isabella held her breath because of his strange reaction, but when his face exploded in excitement, eyes wide and huge smile despite the tear-streaked cheeks. "Sister," he said, breathing in a broken sob, "you here."

Crouching next to him, she put a hand on his shoulder, "Where else would I be, buddy?"

"Mommy said you left," he threw his arms around her, laughing, almost bowling her over in the process.

"Where is she?" Isabella looked around for the thing masquerading as her mother.

"She go walking," he looked around the playground. "I don't like it here."

"Neither do I."

"We go home now." Tucker stood up and grabbed her hand, pulling her toward the gate.

"Afraid not, buddy," it broke her heart to see sad resignation in those bright eyes of his.

"Iee-iee, I don't like it here," he stamped his foot, "spooky."

"I know, it's scary here," Isabella looked at the towering play structure and remembered the time she'd fallen off the regular one as a kid and broken her arm, and she didn't want to imagine what would happen if she fell off this one.

"No," he stomped his foot again, tears returned to his voice, "spooky."

"Okay," she turned and stooped to be eye-level, taking his shoulders in her hands. His eyes darted between her and the gate, barely holding panic in behind his tears. "We're going to get out of here, buddy, but I need you to listen to me very carefully." The ground shook sharply beneath their feet, and Tucker grabbed onto Isabella's neck. "This is a dream, buddy, a nightmare. Do you understand?"

"Mommy said—"

"That's not mommy, not daddy, do you understand me?" Isabella held him out at arms-length and looked into his eyes again.

"Daddy make pancakes," he stammered, unable to understand what Isabella was trying to say. "Breakfast, morning time."

"I know," she insisted, "but it wasn't real."

He looked at her with tears of confusion running down his face, "Real. Pancakes, Mommy, Daddy. Real."

"I want them to be too, buddy," Isabella took a deep breath feeling a tear in the corner of her eyes, but she forged forward, "but they're not. This place is not." The ground beneath them surged more violently, and something boomed in the distance, "We need to get out of here."

"Iee-iee, Iee-iee, spooky."

"I'm here, buddy," she hugged him, "I'm real."

"Spooky," his terror wrenched at her heart. "Corner, spooky, spookies chasing me."

Isabella finally understood what he was trying to tell her and looked over her shoulder to see three shadows flow around the corner a block away from the playground. Isabella grabbed her brother's arm and pulled him toward the gate, her left ankle aching as she slipped on the gravel, falling to her knee. She pushed off, and reaching the gate, she checked where the shadows were. They either hadn't seen her or were headed elsewhere because they passed into the next street.

Trying to find a way to safety, Isabella scanned the playground for anything out of the ordinary. A small grove of pines stood on the opposite side from where she'd arrived; they were dark and gnarled, packed dense with undergrowth, but that anomaly gave her a glimmer of hope. With her brother in tow, Isabella made a break for the grove. If there was a way out, she felt the trees were going to have it. Better the escape was hidden in the strange foreboding trees instead of the impossibly tall play structure. She didn't like the idea of climbing to the top of the ladder with her ankle, and she wasn't sure her brother could climb that high anyway. The trees were her best hope for an escape, and the increasingly shaky ground told her they needed to hurry.

The trees' branches seemed to push back against them, and the air in the too dense undergrowth was thick and hard to breathe. Still, Isabella fought forward anyway, pulling her brother behind her hoping her body moved enough of the brush out of the way to let him pass with relative ease. A couple of times, he yelped as a branch snapped back in his face, but his little legs kept moving in time with her own. When the undergrowth finally broke, Isabella stood under a large canopy, too large for the outside trees. The ground still shook, but she couldn't see the ever-closing clouds on the horizon, which was both a comfort and cause for growing concern.

"Mommy," Tucker yelled, pulling his hand away from Isabella.

"Tucker," the lilt was hollow in the voice coming from her mother's shape, "I thought I told you to stay in the playground."

"Sister came," he beamed up at his mother's face.

"So she did," the thing turned its eyes on Isabella, and the feeling of desperate anger washed over her. "I'm surprised to see you, darling." The last word sounded more like a threat than a term of endearment.

"Tucker and I were just leaving," Isabella bit her bottom lip and took a deep breath in. The thick warm air had taken a chill and thinned in the center of the clearing, and Isabella shivered involuntarily under the gaze of the mother that was not her mother.

"You can't take a child away from its mother, sweetie," she said, bending down to Tucker's level. "Besides, you don't want to leave Mommy, do you, buddy?"

"No," Tucker looked at Isabella, tears beginning to draw clean rivers down the dirt on his cheeks. "I love Mommy."

"And your Mommy loves you too," the thing smiled thinly at Isabella over Tucker's head, "she'd miss you if she never saw you again." That the shadow had spoken the truth was not lost on Isabella, making it was clear this creature was saying more than Tucker could understand. "But I'll let you choose, little man," she shifted her eyes back to Tucker, "do you want to stay here with me or go off with your sister, maybe never seeing me again."

"Iee-iee not do that," his voice smiled.

"She would," the woman insisted. "She would take you away from me."

"Come on, Tucker," Isabella insisted, "we need to get out of here. That's not Mommy."

"Don't I look like Mommy?" Tucker nodded. "Sound like Mommy?" Another nod. Isabella felt her heart snap in two as she realized she would not be able to convince a two-year-old what he saw was not actually true. Lies like that didn't exist in his world yet. "Do you want to stay here with me?" He nodded vigorously, "I need you to tell your sister."

"I stay with Mommy," Tucker said, smiling and hugging the thing in front of him.

"You heard him, Izzy," she motioned to a hole near the base of one of the trees, "there's your door. But this door does not lead you home. You lost the chance when you threw our kindness back in our face."

"Mommy mad?" Tucker asked.

"Not mad," the emotions roiling from her told a different story, "disappointed."

"No," Isabella stood her ground, staring down the woman who wore her mother's face, "I will not leave him here." The strength in her voice surprised her and must have surprised the woman too because she turned Tucker away as if to protect him from danger.

"If you do not leave," she said, "all will be lost. You and your brother will be destroyed, and it will be your fault."

"Not sister's fault," Tucker said, looking at the woman, but she ignored him.

"I won't let that happen," Isabella said, taking a step toward the woman. "I will take him with me."

"That won't save either of you," she took a step back to keep the distance away from Isabella. "You'd think better if you knew where the door leads." The woman pulled Tucker closer to her chest as if he could heal some deep pain she felt. Fear roiled in her eyes.

"It leads away from here," Isabella took another step, matched by the woman, "so it leads to a chance."

"It leads to slaughter," the woman cried out, panic edged the lilt of her mother's voice out of the words. "You will not take him there. He is mine now, and you cannot have him." The desperation in the woman's voice gave Isabella pause. This woman, not a woman, not her mother, this shadow was desperate to protect him, but it felt wrong, and Isabella couldn't stop now.

"You don't know that," Isabella continued walking toward the woman.

"Stop," the woman's voice had changed completely, and Tucker started at the desperate foreign sound, "you don't know what you're doing." The woman was coming unraveled, the tightly controlled emotions were slipping, and Isabella could see darkness beginning to shift around her feet.

"Mommy sad?" Tucker asked, but his voice showed more confusion and worry than concern, and Isabella pushed her advantage.

"Tucker," Isabella tried a different tactic, "Mommy is sad." Isabella met the darkening eyes of the shadow, barely keeping her mother's form. "There is something we can do to make her happy again," tears formed in Isabella's eyes. She had no clue if what she was planning would work, but she needed to try something. The ground constantly rumbled now, and dust began to filter through the air in the clearing. Based on the groaning sounds of wood and metal coming from the other side of the trees, Isabella guessed the edge of the closing trap was getting closer.

"Mommy, happy?" Tucker looked back and forth between Isabella and their mother's face, tears streamed down both.

"Come here, buddy," Isabella held her hand out, "we'll make Mommy happy."

The woman clung tighter to Tucker. The air became thicker with emotions, not only pain and fear from the woman holding Tucker, but sadness, remorse, confusion, and desperation flowed from the trees around Isabella. She could feel three distinct figures closing in from the edges of the forest. Tucker wiggled in the woman's arms. "Make Mommy happy, Iee-iee. Sister happy?" He continued twisting and shimmying out of her arms until they became too insubstantial to hold him, and the searing pain of loss washed through the clearing.

"Let's go," Isabella called, willing Tucker not to look back at the shadow who stood where the woman had been holding him, a shadow bent over as if an ancient wound had been once again ripped open to burn anew. Isabella grabbed Tucker's hand, and without looking around, ran toward the tree which the shadow had motioned to earlier. Near the bottom, a small blue door was tucked into the darkness in a hollow made by exposed roots. Isabella slid the last few feet, scrambling to pull Tucker in front of her and shield him from the confusing emotions pressing on them from all sides.

She kissed his head, then wrenching the door open to the loud cries of voices on the other side, she pushed him through and then dove herself as the falling trees around her began to pull the canopy apart above, revealing a lightless sky.

On the other side of the door, the air was filled with floating gray ash, and hard ash-covered stones scrapped at her knees as she slid to a stop next to her brother. He was standing up, turning slowly, taking in his surroundings, and Isabella, ignoring the pain of her scraped knees and twisted ankle, pulled him into a tight hug and closed her eyes. They were safe, they were out of the trap, and now she needed to get them home.

Opening her eyes to make the next stage of the plan, Isabella's breath caught, and a tsunami of emotions held back momentarily slammed into her senses. Pain, confusion, loss, agony, fear, lots of fear, awash with so many others she could not even begin to separate them, but the emotions weren't what made her blood run cold. Standing around them, what had drawn Tucker's attention, were nine different shadows, all facing away from Isabella and her brother, claws extended and calling out with their ravaged voices as unintelligible, but clearly human, yelling grew louder. A hawk circled above, screeching in defiance, and a lone wolf howled in the distance. Isabella realized she had brought her brother right to the center of the Shadow Congress, the center of the war for a world she knew nothing about but still felt the need to protect.

❧TWENTY-SIX❧

S ister," Tucker whispered before she could stop him, "I scared."

His small voice sounding lost in the tumult still came from farther away than Isabella would have liked, but it was loud enough for one of the shadows to hear him. The full intensity of anger and loss bore down on Isabella as she looked past her brother's tearful face into the darkness facing them. The air seemed to push down on her under the stare of the creature, and she saw her brother's shoulders tighten as he began to tremble.

"Come here, buddy," she whispered, motioning him closer. There was not an inch around them not bathed in shadow, and Isabella knew there was nowhere they could go. The words of the shadow in the trap came back to her, the desperation it felt: *You'd think better if you knew where the door leads.* Isabella wrapped her arms around her brother and pulled him tightly to her. She wrapped her body around him as best she could, protecting him from the shadows with everything she had. Her back tensed, fighting against the overwhelming feeling of loss pouring down on her. Tears began to form in the corners of her eyes, knowing it was only a matter of time before the impending claws raked her back. She pictured those glossy black claws on the insubstantial limbs reaching out for her, waiting to steal her life, her brother's life, and a sob broke from her throat.

The sound of a woman screaming in pain tore through the heavy, dark air. Isabella heard defiance in the cry, which sounded so painful it could only be uttered by someone who was mortally wounded. She thought about Finn and the hunters, of Wren leading the charge against this very hill, against these impossible odds. Her heart broke as the cry came again, closer now, and Isabella imagined this valiant woman fighting her way, wounded, to try and save them. She almost jumped when she felt four small paws land solidly on her back. The same cry at her ear was both terrifying and heartening because now, she knew what it was. In an instant, the back paws pushed off, their claws leaving pinpricks in her back, and the cry receded, taking with it the overbearing loss and anger surging through the shadow.

With one of the shadows out of the circle, the small opening left was enough for Isabella to push her brother through. Looking around at the towering darkness shifting to close the gap, Isabella dove through herself before the eight remaining shadows closed rank at the top of the hill. The emotional toll on the outside was worse than being at the shadow's back, and, for the first time since crossing the river, Isabella felt their loss almost overwhelm her. She put her hands to her head as the pain bore her to her knees. Tucker's small hands grabbed at her as he tried to crawl into her lap for protection.

"Sister," he pleaded, "go now. Spookies here, we go now." Tucker cried into her arms; the weight of the emotions bearing down on them both from these shadows was different from the ones they'd encountered before. Like the one masquerading as her father, they had tendrils whipping around and claws dripping decay on the ground around them.

Her dive through the gap in the shadows, and the subsequent roll down the short hill, caused spurts of ash to float into the air, making her cough and struggle to breathe. She pushed her brother to his feet, hoping he'd run as far as he could, maybe escape this fight or find a hunter to help defend him, but he refused to leave her.

"Sister, stand up," he demanded, stamping his foot in the ashes.

The absurdity of his anger at this moment made her smile despite herself, and she pushed herself up off the ground. The sounds of shouting and fighting raged around her, hunters calling each other and swords swinging through the incorporeal darkness of the shadows. Overhead, Wren's hawk called out and swooped down at something on the other side of the hill before taking to the sky again. Isabella knew she shouldn't, but she had to look at the shadow congress looming on the top of the hill. She could see five of them still standing in their circle, three more having peeled off to chase some attack or another. These wouldn't be killed as easily as the one who'd cornered the child in the woods. She searched them for a weakness, but their bodies were all writhing limbs and swirling darkness.

As she stared at the shadows, one peeled away from the group, leaving four remaining. She watched as the one who left the group spun from the left side to face her and her brother. The bellow it let out echoed through the hillside, causing the ground the shake and ash to pick up in the wind. When it set its dark eyes on her, Isabella's breath caught in her chest, and she felt her muscles tighten as a tremor shot through her body. She would fight this thing for her brother if she had to.

Tracing a line down the hill toward her, the ashes billowed behind it. Tucker pulled on her arm, repeating something over and over again, but Isabella fought the oppressive emotions pouring off the oncoming shadow. "You can't have him," she repeated to herself, louder with each repetition until she was screaming at the descending darkness. Her heart sped up, and her lungs burned. Tears brimmed in her eyes and the world shrank away except for the shadow in front of her. The sounds of the yelling hunters and screech of the hawk had been so loud only moments before but now sounded like they were coming from far away, muted. A shudder shook her body, and the world began to narrow still further.

A flash of gray skidded before her, blocking the view of the shadow, causing the world to crash down once again, the battle, the smell of the ash, her brother's insistent hand on her arm, his halting sobs. She took in a raspy breath, her lungs desperate for air. In front of her, in sharper focus than seemed familiar, Finn was down on one knee, arrow knocked and drawn to his ear. The shadow lunged at him, and from the opposite side, Delson swept in with a curved sword, fatter in the middle than on either end, knocking the shadow's claws away from their target and giving Finn a chance to loose his arrow. The arrow seemed to pass through the shadow, drawing some of the darkness with it only to have it dissipate on the ashen ground.

"Didn't exactly expect you here," he said, knocking another arrow and drawing back to take aim. Delson stood protectively over him, sword held in defense of his fellow hunter.

"Sister?" Tucker's unsure voice behind her, his hand urging her to move, pulled again.

"Found him, I see," he loosed another arrow at the shadow, who swiped with those glossy black claws, cutting it to harmless splinters. He drew another while Delson tried to push back the shadow with his sword.

Isabella looked at the several battles around her. The scene was like nothing she could ever imagine. Groups of people she had seen in the hunter's camp fought against the flailing shadows, driving them back and being driven back in turn. The old fought with as much vigor as Finn and Delson, seemingly ignorant of stiff joints, wielding their canes like swords and clubs. A fierce guttural snarl sounded off to her left as an enormous white wolf with a dark snout, who could only be Vígolfr, crashed through a shadow, tearing away an arm which dissipated before the wolf's paws touched the ground. The shadow turned and swatted the wolf with its remaining arm, a sharp yelp, and the wolf lost its balance and lay stunned on the ground. For a moment, Isabella thought she recognized the man, briefly visible when the shadow turned to attack the prone wolf. The man raised a short gray sword over his head with his left hand, and with a vicious cry, brought it slashing down, cutting the shadow in two. As the shadow dissipated into insubstantial wisps, he rushed to the wolf, heedless of the raging battle the still surrounded them.

"Finn," Isabella found her voice, "I need to get my brother out of here."

"You think," the arrow he loosed flew over Delson's right shoulder and through the arm of the shadow, slowing it enough to let his partner duck under the glistening claws.

"How do I do it?" she asked, desperation clear in her voice. "How do I get him out of here?"

"Weaver's charms, how would I know," he took his eyes off the shadow to shoot her a confused glance, Delson's call brought his attention back to the fight in time to send another arrow through the lower left side. The shadow seemed to stumble before rising again with a shriek making Delson flinch. "Little busy Iz," another arrow drawn back against his ear. "Saw Kimi's move to save your skin. Ask your companion weaver," he released it and knocked another, "if you can find her. Now get outta here, it's not safe for you. Besides," he flashed her a toothy grin and loosed the arrow without looking, it struck the shadow's shoulder, "you can't shoot for nothing."

"Thank you, Finn," Isabella looked at Delson pushing the shadow back away from them. "Thank him too. Be safe."

Finn laughed and took off, running toward Delson and the shadow. "Be safe yourself," he called over his shoulder, "I'm havin' fun."

With a quick scan of the battle around them, Isabella picked a clear path through. She swept her bother into her arms, burying his tear-stained face into her shirt before she ran through the hunters and shadows. A cascade of pain, fear, confusion, loss, and hopelessness all washed over her as they passed the different groups fighting, but nothing seemed directed at them, and they were able to make it to the edge of the ashen landscape. Looking back at the struggling hunters, she saw Wren mixed in with one of the groups going after an enormous shadow towering over them. She was a swirl of blades and limbs, seeming to dance with the shadow, driving it back as she twirled and leaped, silver flashing in the rising sun.

With a silent wish of luck to her friends, Isabella plunged into the vibrant forest heading for the ash tree, hoping the shadows hadn't lied to her about the tree being her way out. Her brother was getting heavy, and her twisted ankle throbbed; they weren't safe, but they were far enough away from the majority of the fighting, and she figured she could set him down.

"We go home," he said, his voice grave, "make Mommy happy. Sister happy."

"Yes, buddy, that's where we're going," Isabella looked around for the canopy of the giant ash tree, "I just need to find—"

The shrieking call sounded like a woman being hurt echoed through the forest, followed by a bellow filled with anger and loss. Isabella stopped in her tracks. She looked at her brother and back the way the sound came.

"Kimi," Isabella said the name under her breath, then looked back at the brother. "I just need to check something first."

"Fuzzy in trouble?" He asked, looking into the woods where she was looking.

"Could be," she put a hand on each shoulder, "I need you to follow me closely and be very quiet. Can you do that?"

He nodded vigorously and set his jaw with a surprising amount of determination for his age, but his eyes told the real story as they darted around the trees like they would reach out and drag him away. "Close," he said and grabbed the hem of Isabella's shirt.

Isabella didn't like bringing him deeper into the forest, off the path, but she also didn't want to leave him on the trail by himself. The call came again, and Isabella picked her way quickly through the thickening underbrush. Prickers tore at her skin, and twice she heard her brother whimper behind her, but his hand never left the hem of her shirt. She broke through the undergrowth, and a high-pitched, shrieking sound came from the forest to her right, and immediately she turned. Rounding the edge of a bush, Isabella saw a small red fox cowering under a tree stump. She was cornered, and a shadow loomed over her.

Without giving it a second thought, Isabella grabbed a branch from the ground and, yelling at the top of her lungs, hurled it at the shadow. The throw was utterly pathetic, even by her standards, and the stick went left and fell about three feet short of the shadow, but it accomplished what she wanted. The shadow turned on her, the loss almost palpable, but Isabella stood her ground. She wasn't about to let Kimi down again, not after everything Kimi had done for her despite the way she'd treated the beautiful fox. She may never get her forgiveness or become a dreamweaver, but she would not let anything happen to Kimi if she could help it.

Seeing Isabella and her brother, the shadow rose to its full height filling the area under the trees with writhing limbs and swirling darkness. This time, as she saw in her periphery a flash of red move out from under the stump, a shimmer of something almost solid in the darkness of the shadow's chest caught her eye. The sound of Kimi's escape through the leaf-strewn forest floor made the shadow bellow at the loss of its prey, and with one last menacing look at Isabella, it tore off, noiselessly, through the forest after Kimi.

Isabella knew she couldn't take Tucker to chase after the shadow, it would be too dangerous for him, but she also knew without her help, Kimi was doomed. Standing there, watching the settling leaves on the ground, the dappled sunlight was blotted out as a large shadow overtook her from behind without her knowing. Steeling herself for the emotional onslaught she knew was coming, Isabella turned around, pulling her brother behind her to protect him. Looking up at what stood in front of her, Isabella let out the breath she'd been holding and laughed. The big smiling face of Ajay looked down on the pair of them with sheer joy.

"Finn's *yaar*," he swept her up in his arms, the blush of exertion clear on his face. "Found your brother then? First class."

"Finn's what?"

"*Yaar, beedu,* friend." He put her down and ruffled Tucker's hair, then looking over her shoulder, "Bad business, that."

She looked back into the woods, "Kimi's in trouble," Isabella set her jaw and narrowed her eyes as she looked in the direction Kimi had fled, "I need to help her."

"No wonder Finn took a liking to you," his rumble of a laugh sounded warm and safe, "you're both completely *satkela.*"

"I need to help her," Isabella looked from Tucker to Ajay.

"Right," Ajay nodded, all joking clearly gone from his face, "go, I'll watch the boy," he placed a beefy hand on Tucker's shoulder and drew a long thin knife from his belt with the other.

Tucker looked up at the giant of a man next to him, cocked his head to the side, and eyes went wide with shock, "You really big."

"And you're really small little man," Ajay said, a grin and a chuckle in his voice.

"You fight with that thing?" Isabella pointed to the knife he held in his hand.

The question drew a belly laugh from the smiling man, "This toothpick? No little weaver," he said, eyeing her carefully. "If you are going after the shadow chasing your *lomri,* you're going to need more than sticks. Especially with your arm." He held the knife out to Isabella.

"Thank you, Ajay," Isabella said, looking at the knife in her hands. It was clearly something made for a fighter because the weight was almost twice what the fishing knife had been. The metal of the blade was a lustrous silver color with symbols carved in the sides. The handle was made of a luminescent dark that danced in the dappled light of the morning, set in the base of the handle, a bright yellow stone whose facets caught the light and multiplied within itself, making the stone seem to glow with inner power. "I will be sure to return this to you when I get back."

"No little weaver," he shook his head, "you will need that."

"Why do you keep calling me that? Little weaver."

"I've been around a while," he said with a wink, "I know what I see. Now go save your companion. *Abhi saltale*, weaver, fix what needs fixing."

Tucker grabbed Ajay's finger with his little hand, causing the big man to start. "Go Iee-iee," he said, "save fuzzy."

Isabella chewed her lip as she looked at the two of them through narrowed eyes. Then with a look of resolute joy, she winked, pivoted on her right foot, and jogged off into the forest.

TWENTY-SEVEN

Isabella stopped to catch her breath, leaning against a tree, the peeling white bark cool and smooth against her sweating palm. Her left ankle throbbed, but Isabella knew she needed to keep pushing forward. She'd just broken through thick underbrush along the forest floor into a small wildlife trail. Clearly, Kimi scurried under the brush, hoping to slow the shadow down, but the tickets didn't even look disturbed. Isabella assumed the shadow was able to just pass through the obstructions. She was the only one who needed to slash her way through the branches. Kimi had been through here, she was positive because the ground had been torn up in several places where she had made sharp turns, presumably to avoid the shadow's slashes. There were also lines of ash through several areas, a clear indication the shadow had been through here. She had been crashing through the underbrush, heedless of the noise she was making, and Isabella just hoped she would get there in time.

The sound of Kimi's scream echoed through the forest again, followed by the other high pitched shrieking. Isabella pushed off of the waving birch tree and headed in the direction of the cries. A sudden yelp made her blood run cold; ignoring the throbbing pain in her ankle and shooting up her leg, Isabella charged through the thicket and breaking out the other side, the scene unfolding in front of her stopped her in her tracks. Kimi had her tail down and her ears back, and she was emitting a guttural noise accompanied by spitting saliva and bared teeth. Her eyes were wild and deadly, and favoring her right back paw, she backed into a crook made by two fallen branches from an old hawthorn tree.

The shadow seemed to have grown in size since Isabella had seen it last. It filled the area in front of Kimi, allowing Isabella to catch glimpses of the little fox only occasionally through the shifty darkness of the shadow's body. Intensifying emotions of loss and anger flowed from the shadow, but now confusion and fear mixed with them, all falling off the shadow standing between her and Kimi. Isabella marveled at how the fox could keep her composure when facing the emotional onslaught head-on, but she didn't have time to think about it much. It was clear without action, there was no way for Kimi to escape the situation.

Isabella closed her eyes and carefully drew the dagger Ajay had given her. Steadying her breath like Finn had taught her with the bow, she lunged at the back of the shadow. If she could connect with the solid center in the shadow, she was sure it would at least dislodge the shadow, if not destroy it. Two steps across the small opening, Isabella landed with her left foot on a fallen branch, further wrenching her ankle and causing pain to shoot up her leg into her lower back. Her swing went wide, instead only catching a piece of one of the smaller tentacles. Isabella overbalanced with the strike, dropped the knife, and landed hard on her right shoulder. When she hit the ground, a grinding noise combined with the sharp pain radiating from the shoulder told Isabella there was clearly a problem. The knife had drawn some of the shadow away from the creature, but it barely flinched.

The shadow continued its advance on Kimi undisturbed. Isabella took a deep breath, her right arm felt weak, and there was a bulge in the front of her shoulder. Wincing with the pain of each jarring movement, Isabella struggled to her knees, grasping the knife clumsily in her left hand and pressing the beautiful craftsmanship into the dirt to help her stand with only one usable arm. With hobbling painful steps, steps which seemed to take more effort than they should have, Isabella lurched between the shadow and the fox, blocking Kimi's body from the swinging claws of the shadow with her body.

The emotions emanating from the shadow seemed muted in the face of Isabella's physical pain, allowing her to focus enough to block the incoming claws with the small knife in her left hand. The shadow reared up and let loose a mournful cry with more emotion in it than Isabella had ever experienced. It cut through the pain in her shoulder and beat at her heart. The loss was almost palpable. She felt the deepest pain and sorrow loss could bring, gut-wrenching hopelessness when all you lived for is ripped away, and for a moment, Isabella's knees bowed, and it looked like she would collapse to the ground.

Images flooded her mind, a small boy, not much older than Tucker, laughing and holding a delicate older hand. The eyes left the boy to respond to some muffled words behind them. Then eyes back to the hand, fingers holding an empty glove. Panic, loss, fear, confusion cycled through her. Tears rose unbidden to her eyes, and she looked into the eyes of the shadow. The hollow darkness there told a story different from the emotions pulsing around the clearing. The eyes called for help. They were the eyes of someone trapped in their worst nightmare with no hope of escape.

Taken aback by the unexpected emotions, Isabella stood gazing into the creature's eyes, trying to make sense of it all. Lost in the emotion flooding from the shadow, Isabella forgot about her ankle and took a step forward. As her weight landed on the twisted ankle, she flinched, quickly shifted her weight to the right ankle, and reached down, instinctively, to protect her wounded side. As she did, a breeze pushed her hair to the side. Isabella hadn't noticed the shining claws raise up and descend, intent on spreading their corruption. She looked down at Kimi, who had taken the shadow's distraction to get out into the open and winding up at Isabella's side. The fox trembled and favored its leg, but she was barking and spitting, refused to back down against the onslaught of the coming shadow.

With the knife in her left hand, her right one hanging uselessly by her side, Isabella took a swipe at the shadow's chest. The dagger passed through the shadow, drawing out a thin trail as it came through the other side. She knew she would never succeed in whittling this thing down. She needed a big hit. Turning the knife blade down in her hand, Isabella took one final swipe at the creature in front of her. She overbalanced and tumbled forward, landing hard on her right shoulder again and, ignoring the searing pain, managed to roll several feet away from the Shadow. The pain lanced through her, and her vision narrowed. Nausea roiled in her stomach, and every inch of her body ached.

Kimi backed away, still hissing and spitting, trying to lure the shadow away from Isabella's prone body, but the shadow didn't take the bait. Isabella tried pushing herself off the ground, but the pain in her now throbbing right shoulder sent flashes through her field of vision, causing her to fall back to the ground, pinning the dagger beneath her. The new lances of pain threatened to shatter the snatches of a plan even as they began to form. She could feel the loss and anger rising as the shadow approached. Frantically, she searched with her left arm for a stick or rock, knowing she would only have one chance to get this right. Isabella knew the plan was a long shot at best, it relied on Kimi distracting the shadow long enough for her to take action, but she had no way to communicate this to Kimi. She had to trust the little fox would do what she always did, try to help.

Kimi didn't disappoint. With a spray of dirt from the speed at which the fox stopped next to Isabella's head, Isabella's heart beat quicker, a feat she hadn't known was previously possible given how fast it had been beating before. "What are you doing girl," Kimi scolded, "get up and fight."

Isabella's hand closed around a sizable rock. She hoped it would be enough.

There was a grating sound resembling laughter, and when the shadow spoke, the pain and loss Isabella felt emanating from it came through clearly in the voice. "She knows there is no point, you foolish creature. This is where your journey ends. You are both wounded. I will put your misery to an end. He would have liked you," the shadow seemed to pulse momentarily, "I'll send you to him." The shadow lunged toward Kimi, who, pushing off with her uninjured leg, managed to barely miss the creature's claws. Isabella rolled over on her back and threw the rock at the shadow, aiming at a small darker spot, stationary at the center of the roiling black mass. The rock went high and right, passing harmlessly through the shadow, a dissipating black line following it out the back. The shadow turned its attention back to the prone girl.

A rustling in the bushes behind the shadow drew Kimi's attention, and Isabella, still with her left arm outstretched, followed Kimi's gaze. "Tucker," she cried out, her voice torn with emotion, toward the rustling, "I told you to stay with Ajay."

The shadow cackled and, without needing to turn, inverted itself to face the sound. Rushing at the bushes in hopes of a defenseless victim to intensify the pain for the others. Isabella noticed Kimi's muscles tensing and lowered her hand to the fox's back. Their eyes met, Kimi's expressing a ferocious protective instinct while Isabella's sparked with mischief. The confused fox relaxed slightly and watched Isabella struggle to her feet and pick up the dagger by the blade with her left hand.

The shadow reached the other side of the clearing only to find a rock at the base of a bush. Letting out a shriek that would make a banshee cower in fear and slashing its claws, shredding the bush and scattering now decaying branches and leaves through the clearing, the shadow inverted again and rushed at Isabella and Kimi, black tendrils flying behind it like windsocks in a hurricane.

Kimi pulled on Isabella's pant leg, "We need to go," the fox begged, "Izzy, we can't take her by ourselves."

Isabella stood as if transfixed by the shadow. She ignored the fox's pleas and searched the approaching darkness with her eyes. She knew if she could find the spot, the heart of darkness, she would have one chance. Kimi looked up at her from the ground and yipped but wouldn't run. Isabella knew now running from a fight was something Kimi didn't do. She took a breath to steady herself in the rushing emotions threatening once again to overwhelm her and mumbled something under her breath.

Her eyes lighted on the spot when the shadow was halfway across the clearing, and time seemed to stretch out. Drawing her left arm back even with her ear, Isabella waited another moment. Closer is better, she said to herself, knowing there would only be one chance to get this right. Taking a deep breath and exhaling, like Finn had explained with the bow, Isabella flung her arm forward and let go of the blade as her arm was pointing at the spot she had her eye on. The knife flew, end over end, and the shadow raced toward the now unarmed pair, claws outstretched dripping lines of decay below the long glistening nails. There was a slight popping sound when the two met, and at first, nothing changed.

Then, everything changed. The tip of the blade pierced the dark heart of the shadow, the expression on the face dissolved from one of confusion and pain to one of relief. As the shadow dissipated and the emotions of loss and anger began to fade, Isabella could finally see the purpose behind the look on the shadow's face, it was fleeting, but it was clearly there. Behind the swirling darkness, a woman momentarily materialized inside the shadow before the entire thing disappeared. Her face was smooth and young, and her eyes held the knowledge of loss and pain, but they also held relief and acceptance. The woman's face smiled briefly at Isabella before the shadow fully dissolved, taking the image of the woman with it.

Isabella stood looking at the empty air in front of her and felt herself physically relax as the air around her, previously charged with so many negative emotions, seemed to exhale them all at once, leaving in their place a calm pervading the area. Her shoulder and ankle throbbed, but Isabella felt in control for the first time since her brother had disappeared. Turning around, she looked down at Kimi. The little fox was leaning against a small tree but visibly more relaxed. Her eyes were beginning to take on the intelligence Isabella had always seen there, the animalistic wildness which had supplanted it being no longer needed.

"That was impressive," Kimi said, looking at Isabella with what appeared to be the fox's approximation of a smile but looked more like exhaustion.

"Softball in gym class," Isabella shrugged.

"Softball is played with knives?"

"No," she chuckled and walked over to pick up her dagger, which had stuck, blade first into the ground. Something looked different about the jewel on its end, but Isabella decided it was a mystery for another time. Right now, she needed to check on Kimi. "Are you alright?" Isabella came over and crouched down to get a closer look at Kimi.

"I've been better," Kimi turned to the side, showing a broad white line spread across the right haunch. "The thing got me." She tried to take a step but collapsed in the process.

Isabella placed her hand near the fox's leg and felt and burning heat radiating from her cut. "Kimi," he eyes wide, "what can I do?"

"Afraid there's not much you can do," Kimi tried to lick her wound but flinched away at the smell of it. "Nombeko might have something or a caretaker, but they are not here, and I won't be walking anymore, it seems."

"You're giving up?"

"Under a hawthorn tree is not a bad place to go," Kimi said, looking up at the twisted branches above her. "Thank you for saving me," she must have noticed Isabelle's pained face. "You have saved me. Even if I do not live to see the setting sun, the shadow would have done worse. We are even now. You can go back to your world and live your life. I am sorry we couldn't have made this work. You might have made a good dreamweaver."

Isabella put the knife into its sheath and crouched down next to Kimi, slipping her left arm under the little red fox's middle.

"What are you doing?"

"We are nowhere near even," she said through gritted teeth as she stood. Fighting through the pain, and began to carry Kimi back to the ash tree's outer branches, hoping Ajay might know how to help. Each step brought a new feeling of pain, deep and throbbing. Isabella had never felt so weak, and yet she'd never been so sure of her choices as she was right now.

"Wait," Kimi said from where her head rested on Isabella's shoulder.

"No time," Isabella knew she couldn't carry Kimi much farther, but she would go as long as she could, maybe she could make it, "have to keep going."

"No, stop," Kimi's voice was weak but insistent, so giving herself a rest, Isabella obliged and set the maimed fox on a soft bed of leaves. "In the hollow of the tree."

Looking to where Kimi had pointed with her nose, Isabella saw clear signs of a bees' nest, an active one given the amount of traffic going in and out of it. "That?" she asked, "Those bees?"

"Honey is a natural antiseptic," Kimi explained. "The hunters use it, some of the keepers too in their charms." She covered her face with her paws, "Never mind," she continued, "too dangerous. Best to get you and Tucker back to safety."

Isabella watched the bees flying in and out of the nest. "Will it help?" she asked without taking her eyes off of the gathering swarm.

"Don't worry about it," Kimi said, flinching as the pain clearly intensified, "find Nombeko."

Turning her eyes to the fox, Isabella considered her for a moment, then shaking her head, "No time, is there?"

"Could be," Kimi looked past her at the nest as well, "but if you try to get the honey from the nest, they will swarm."

"And I'll be stung," she looked around searching the ground for something to help, "I'm not allergic, I'll be fine."

"With that many bees, you don't have to be allergic."

"Then I guess we just have to be smart," she said, grabbing a hand full of twigs and wet leaves from the ground around her. Kimi looked on as Isabella gathered sticks and branches and a pile of wet leaves. Leaving the leaves to the side, she carefully leaned the sticks together, smaller pieces on the bottom, and getting progressively larger. "All those family camping trips are going to pay off after all," she added, pulling at the hem on her shirt, worrying some of the areas ripped or frayed by the prickers she pushed through during the chase until she was able to get a strip about an inch wide to tear loose.

"A fire?" Kimi asked. "I'm not sure destroying the tree will be helpful."

"Next to the tree," Isabella explained while she continued working. "Once I get it going, I'll put the leaves on, and the smoke should make the bees lethargic."

"They'll still sting you."

"Yup," Isabella smiled over her shoulder and pulled out the dagger Ajay had given her. She tested a few rocks around her until she found one that would spark. After several tries, the piece of her shirt caught, then the wood went up shortly after. Her plan worked well enough, she was still stung five times, but she could get the honey and smear it on Kimi's leg. The infection began to bubble like they did when her mom would pour hydrogen peroxide on cuts at home. Satisfied she'd done what she could, Isabella scooped up Kimi and limped through the forest.

After a while, Kimi squirmed and asked to be put down. Worried, Isabella set her down, and the fox, tentatively at first, began to limp along next to Isabella. As relief soared in her, Isabella and Kimi broke the last collection of underbrush separating them from Ajay and Tucker. Isabella smiled at the two of them. Tucker had gotten Ajay to sit on the ground with him and was trying to teach the big man to play patty-cake. Seeing Ajay sitting there, repeating the words with her brother warmed her heart, and she looked down at Kimi, who leaned gently against her right leg for support as they stood looking at the two, not wanting to disrupt their game.

TWENTY-EIGHT

S itting cross-legged on the ground, Ajay looked like a giant. His massive body was hunched over slightly to reach the starkly smaller Tucker, their hands clapping out a rhythm Isabella had done with her brother countless times. *Patty-cake, patty-cake, baker's man–* A smile, matching the man in size, shone on his face. The moment the big man saw them, his skin went instantly flushed, and he jumped to his feet against the cries of his small friend and, raising his hands over his head, bellowed, "Little weaver, you're back." He whisked over to Isabella, leaving Tucker getting up from the ground by himself. "I see you did what was needed." He smiled at the two standing there, utterly ignorant to their wounds.

Isabella stood leaning heavily on a tree trunk for her part, watching the two of them with a sad smile. She was happy her brother was safe, and he would be going home soon, but she had grown attached to this place and these people in her short time here. This was something bigger than herself: people willing to risk everything for the opportunity to do the right thing. Her experience killing the shadow haunted her. The feeling of gratitude had emanated from the shadow as it dissipated hadn't been anticipated. Isabella nodded at Ajay's words and let him scoop her up into a big hug, wincing only slightly as he squeezed her arm.

"You are injured," he said, putting her down, "I'll help." He grabbed her arm, pausing for a moment as if just remembering something, "This will hurt." Ajay smiled apologetically and put one large hand just under her swollen joint, and grabbed her wrist with the other. He pulled down and out while simultaneously pushing on her body. Isabella screamed as she heard the pop of the shoulder going back into the socket. The pain lessened almost immediately to a dull ache. The large man smiled apologetically, "It would have been worse to leave it."

"Thanks, Ajay," she said, patting him on the arm with her left hand, "it does feel better."

"Sister," Tucker rushed over to her side and hugged her leg. "Sister arm hurt? Sit down," he pulled her forward by her uninjured hand to a soft patch of moss he'd been sitting on. "I rub your back. Feel better?"

Isabella lowered herself to the ground, wincing as she jarred her ankle accidentally. Tucker walked over, and with childish seriousness, began to rub gentle circles on her back. Kimi limped over after them and, pausing briefly, climbed onto

Isabella's lap and curled into a little ball of red fur. Isabella let her good arm gently stroke the fox's matted coat, and a sense of peace or rightness washed over her.

Ajay stood watching the three of them, hands on his hips, smiling. "This," he said simply and nodded his head, smiling knowingly.

After soaking in the peaceful air under the bows of the ash tree, Isabella cleared her throat. "Time to get home," she looked down the path behind her toward where Finn and the others presumably still fought the shadow congress.

"They will be fine," Ajay said softly. "I will join them when you are on your way."

"Can I ask you a favor first?" Isabella looked down at the now resting fox. "Kimi was injured by the shadow, scratched on her back thigh. We spread honey on it, she said it could help," the red fluff in her lap shifted and groaned a little, "but she needs someone to do something for her."

"Honey," he looks at them, clearly impressed, "that'll do in a pinch, but I will take her to Nigel. He'll do her up right. Don't you worry for your companion. The honey, did it bubble?"

"Yeah," Isabella hugged Tucker, who'd stopped rubbing her back and walked next to her, resting his head on her shoulder.

"Good that," he nodded again. "Probably saved her life with that one."

Isabella smiled and looked around her, then sighed. She'd dealt with all of the loose ends, except saying goodbye to Finn and the others, but they had been away for long enough as it was, and she needed to get her brother back home. She couldn't wait for the battle to end. Besides, her brother needed to get to safety, and it wasn't her fight. "Why are you here? Don't get me wrong, I appreciate the fact you were. I'm not sure what I would have done if you weren't," Isabella looked from Ajay to Kimi and back. "But shouldn't you be off fighting the shadow congress with the rest of the hunters."

"We all have our roles to play, little weaver," he smiled back at her. "Finn asked me to keep an eye out for you when the fighting started, something about you always showing up at the worst times. I saw Kimi was in trouble, figured I'd help same as you. Companions are important to the weavers. I figured helping yours was helping you."

"Thank you," she said, bowing her head in exhaustion, "for everything."

"Iee-iee," Tucker said, the exhaustion evident in his voice, "go home now? Make Mommy happy, you promised."

"I did, buddy," Isabella squeezed her eyes shut, "I just wish I knew how."

"Weaver's charms," Ajay burst out, "you mean to tell me after all this you don't know how to get yourself home? I thought all weavers just knew."

"What does that even mean, weaver's charms? Finn kept saying it. I've never heard it before. I just figured it was one of those weird things he said," Isabella's frustration was brimming under the surface again. "Is it, or does it actually mean something?"

"I don't know for sure. People around here use it when something is hard to believe," he looked up at the branches over their head as if trying to remember something, "but stories I've heard say some weavers, maybe all of them, have charms to help them in their missions. Usually, they're earned from the Council of Dreamers at the capitol, but there are other ways. Caretakers sometimes have them, peddlers. Not sure how much stock to put in that, stories and all, but Finn'd swear by 'em," he smiled at the look of concern crossing Isabella's face at the mention on Finn. "Don't worry about that boy. He's tougher than he puts on. Saved my skin more than once. He'll come through this."

"I don't have any ch—" Isabella remembered the dream catcher she'd gotten from the old woman back in Swift River. "These caretakers, what are they like?"

"Not sure they're like anything special. Peddlers. They have bags or carts they push around selling trinkets and such. Most are crazy, *satkela*."

Isabella stood up, gently placing the groggy Kimi on the ground. She stretched and yawned, looking more exhausted than in danger of dropping dead. The honey had left a sticky mess on her hand quarter, but the cut looked normal now, and except for a white swath or fir running down the upper part of her left leg, the infection or corruption seemed to be gone, and Isabella smiled softly at her.

"I was comfortable," she grumbled before going over to sit by Tucker, who squealed with delight and bent down to pet her. She licked his hand, then turned her attention back to Isabella, watching her curiously.

Sticking a hand into her pocket, Isabella pulled out the dreamcatcher she'd gotten from the old woman in the market place and looked at it. Something was different about the light filtering through the ash tree branches and dancing within the crystals hanging from the delicate leather webs. She looked back at everyone, "Weaver's charms?" She shrugged her shoulders and tossed the dreamcatcher toward the trunk of the tree. It seemed to catch in the air and began to spin, the crystals throwing light around the middle until it expanded into what looked like a passageway.

"I'll be a rumbly muppet," Ajay said behind her. "Finn's going to be so jealous."

Isabella walked back and knelt before Kimi, "I'm sorry for how I treated you. I get it now what you did. Every time you were trying to help me, but I wouldn't let you. I'm sorry, and I owe you more than I could possibly repay." The fox sat up straighter and seemed to smile a little. Isabella kissed her on the top of her head, then stood up, holding her uninjured arm out to Tucker. He grabbed her hand and stared wide-eyed at the still swirling circle of light. Inside they could see a green pine forest. A light rain seemed to be falling on the other side, and with one last look back, Isabella led Tucker through the opening and into the pine forests she knew surrounded her neighborhood.

Passing over the portal's threshold sounded like walking through a wind tunnel. Instantly, Isabella and Tucker stood in the middle of the woods in their neighborhood, three blocks from their house. She could see the backs of people's homes and smell the smoke from people's wood stoves. The birds sang in the light drizzle falling on them both.

"Home now?" Tucker asked, looking up at his sister.

Isabella looked around nervously. She was fooled before, but the birds' singing and the smell of the rain put her at ease. She felt the ornate knife Ajay had given her weighing down the pocket of her jacket as she reached down and picked up the dreamcatcher sitting in the leaves at her feet. "Home now," she said, relief flooding her voice as she squeezed her brother's hand tightly in her own. Together, they limped to the forest's edge and began toward the playground and, past that, their home.

There were not many cars on the road in the early hours of the morning, so Isabella assumed it must be Saturday. Otherwise, her neighbors would be heading to work or church, but Saturdays started slowly in the neighborhood. For a moment, fear fluttered in her stomach that this was not the real world. Somehow she'd fallen back into a trap from the shadows. Still, as they neared the playground, everything was back to the way it was supposed to be, and the fluttering in Isabella's stomach slackened.

The fluttering didn't entirely disappear until she pushed open the gate to their front walkway and the front door of her house flew open. Her mother, tears streaming down her face, ran down the walk and swept her children into her arms, sobbing into Isabella's already damp hair. Her father, more restrained but clearly relieved at the sight of both his children safely home, followed after her and, placing a reassuring hand on Isabella's shoulder, gave his customary squeeze and kissed the top of her head before ushering them all back into the house.

When they first got in the house, the flurry of activity was a bit overwhelming to Isabella after everything she'd been through. After checking her wounds and having some cookies her mother had stress-baked, her father ushered Tucker upstairs for a bath and made Izzy sit on the couch with her sore ankle raised on a pillow. Through all of this, her mother never left her side.

"Izzy," her mother said when she finally could say anything other than you're back, "you scared me when you ran off," she pulled Isabella into her arms for yet another hug, still wiping the tears from her face, "I don't know how you found him, but thank you, thank you, thank you, and never do that again. I was just so worried."

"I'm sorry, Mom," it felt good to be able to rely on her parents again, "I just needed to find him."

"I know, honey," she said. "Your father is putting Tucker down now, back in his room too. Repairmen came while you were missing. Your father had scheduled the repair before everything happened, and I just never even thought about it. Lucky Mrs. Orbison from next door was over when they came. I almost sent them away, but she insisted. I don't know if I could have handled it without her here. I was just so–"

"We're back, Mom." Isabella pulled her mother into a hug this time, "We're okay."

"I know, baby," she said.

"Just got off the phone with the police," Isabella's father walked down the stairs, "they're going to want to talk to you, Izzy.

I told them they need to wait until tomorrow because you need to rest tonight."

"And see a doctor," her mother interjected. "You're limping, and your shoulder looks bad."

"But before any of that," her father insisted, "rest. I'll take her up to bed hun, why don't you call the grandparents and let them know the kids are home. You know they're going to want to hear."

"Good idea," she hugged Isabella one more time, "I just love you so much, baby. You know that, right?"

"I do," Isabella watched her mother walk into the kitchen and listened for a moment as her lilting voice began to talk into the phone. Then she turned to her father. He stood leaning on the banister and watched at her with a strange smile on his face.

Putting his hand under her left arm, he began to help her up the stairs. They were in her room before he said anything. He sat her down on her bed carefully and then sat next to her. "Before you get some sleep, I need to ask you something."

"What's wrong, Daddy?"

"Nothing's wrong," he smiled an odd smile again, "I just need to know," he paused as if trying to figure out how to say what he wanted to say. "Have you met Vígolfr?"

Isabella didn't know how to respond; this was the last question she had expected her father to ask. She thought back to the white wolf on the frozen lake. It felt like so long ago. He'd told her about Kimi, about rescuing her brother. He'd set her on the quest, which helped bring them both home. "How do you–"

she struggled to get the words out past her confusions, "How do you know him?"

A smile grew on her father's serious face. In it, Isabella could see pride and happiness, but she still didn't understand any of what he was trying to say. "I'll explain tomorrow, Cricket," he said, standing up from her bed and fluffing her pillow like he used to do every night.

"It was you," she said, as the pieces fell into place, "you were—"

He raised his eyebrow at her and smiled. "We'll figure out a story for your mom and the police in the morning. For now, don't worry about anything. You're safe. And since now we know," he kissed the top of her head, "we are going to need to train you." He walked to the door and stopped, shaking his head and smiling back at her. "Just think, my daughter, a Dreamweaver." He chuckled and then left the room to head downstairs.

Isabella sat there for a few minutes. She tried to make sense of what he'd just said, about Vígolfr, training, being a dreamweaver. She wanted to run downstairs and make him explain more, but she was just so tired, and her bed so inviting after the ordeal she'd been through. Isabella figured there was always tomorrow. She lay her head down on the pillow and drifted off into a dreamless sleep.

Thank you for joining Isabella on her journey into the dream world. Don't worry, there is more to the story yet to unfold.

Keep your eye out for the next installment of Izzy and Kimi's adventures in Dreamweaver Diaries BOOK TWO:

DEPTHS OF THE REBELS' STONE

Until then, sign up for my mailing list so you don't miss the updates, and get access to the official ***Dreamweaver Diaries Choose-Your-Own-Adventure*** to discover if you have what it takes to become a Dreamweaver!

www.ericjohnsonwriter.com

ABOUT THE AUTHOR

Eric Johnson spends his days chasing after one of those diabolically bipedal entities we often refer to with the innocuous moniker of "Pre-Schooler" or waking in the wee hours of the morning to quiet someone's nightmares or weave them a pleasant dream. Otherwise, he is correcting papers, planning lessons, climbing trees, remodeling his home in the woods, reading in the groggy wastes of the middle of the night (since those aforementioned entities don't sleep), or drinking black, dark roast (or something with a little more bite). Sometimes he even get some writing in there too.

You can also read his poetry in a full-length collection titled *The Conditions We Live*, published by Unsolicited Press.

To find out more about Eric and his work, or sign up for the mailing list at ericjohnsonwriter.com.

www.ingramcontent.com/pod-product-compliance
Lightning Source LLC
Chambersburg PA
CBHW071502110726
47908CB00003B/694